THE INFERNAL CURSE

RITE WORLD: BLACKTHORN HUNTERS
ACADEMY BOOK 5

JULIANA HAYGERT

COPYRIGHT

This book is a work of fiction. Names, characters, places, and incidents either are products of the author's imagination or are used fictitiously. Any resemblance to actual persons, living or dead, events, or locales is entirely coincidental.

Copyright © 2020 by Juliana Haygert

All rights reserved. This book or any portion thereof may not be reproduced or used in any manner whatsoever without the express written permission of the publisher except for the use of brief quotations in a book review.

Manufactured in the United States of America.

First Edition January 2020

www.JulianaHaygert.com

Edited by H. Danielle Crabtree

Cover design by Covers by Juan

Any trademark, service marks, product names, or names featured are the property of their respective owners, and are used only for reference. There is no implied endorsement if one of these terms is used.

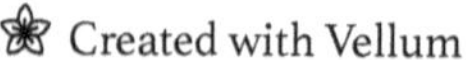 Created with Vellum

AUTHOR'S NOTE

I hope you enjoy reading *The Infernal Curse*!

Don't forget to sign up for my Newsletter to find out about new releases, cover reveals, giveaways, and more!

If you want to see exclusive teasers, help me decide on covers, read excerpts, talk about books, etc, join my reader group on Facebook: Juliana's Club!

RITE WORLD

Welcome to the RITE WORLD!

Rite World:
The Vampire Heir (Book 1)
The Witch Queen (Book 2)
The Immortal Vow (Book 3)
The Warlock Lord (Book 4)
The Wolf Consort (Book 5)
The Crystal Rose (Book 6)
The Wolf Forsaken (Book 7)
The Fae Bound (Book 8)
The Blood Pact (Book 9)

Rite World: Blackthorn Hunters Academy
The Demons Kiss (Book 1)
The Hunter Secret (Book 2)
The Soul Bond (Book 3)
The Shadow Trials (Book 4)
The Immortal Vow (Book 5)

MAP

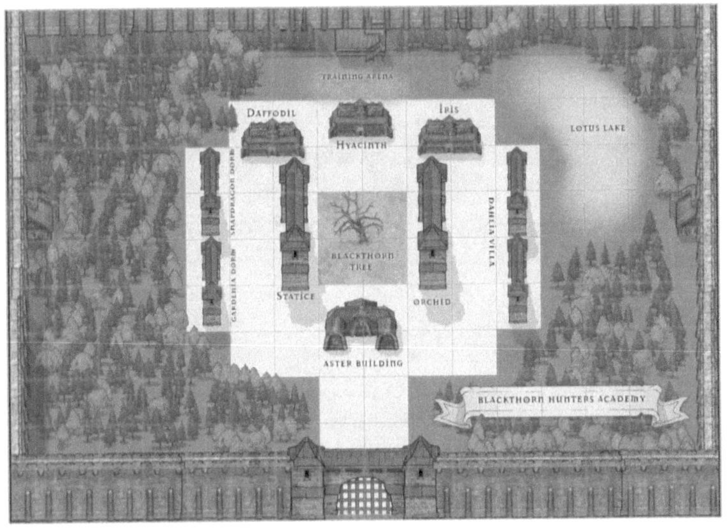

Map of Blackthorn Hunters Academy

Click here to view the map in a separate browser.

1

Our meeting was interrupted one too many times.

First, it was Karen bickering about Kristin's participation in whatever we were planning. Then, it was Jasmin talking about her piece of the underworld—which was what had been promised to her when she joined us. Tanner complained that we hadn't made much progress in the months he had been away, though it seemed he hadn't either.

We also had calls from Ava's father, asking her to leave the academy, and a visit from Professor Eleanor, Harvey's mother, who was intent on taking her son home.

"I'm not going, Mom," Harvey snapped. "I'm going to stay and help anyway I can."

"Help? Help with what?" Professor Eleanor turned her grave eyes to my mother. "Martha, please, what the hell is going on here?"

My mother stared at her friend of many years. "Eleanor, Brikan won't stop. He'll come after Erin and the others." My mother gestured to my half-sisters. "He'll destroy everything in his path. Before he can do that, we need to take the fight to him. We need to defeat him."

Professor Eleanor gawked at my mother. "Have you gone insane?"

My mother guided Professor Eleanor out of the headmaster's office, and closed the door behind them. Even so, we heard most of their argument.

"No matter what she says, I'm not going." Harvey crossed his arms. "This is my choice."

Though my mood was dark and my heart was wilting, I offered him a small smile. Thank goodness he was staying. If he, or any of my friends left, I wasn't sure I could do this alone.

A moment later, the shouting stopped and my mother entered the room again.

"So?" I asked, afraid Professor Eleanor and the Blackthorn Hunters would take back their decision of making my mother the new headmaster.

"I convinced her to leave—for now," my mother said. She turned to Harvey. "But she won't give up. I'm sure she'll see you later, or even come back and try to drag you home."

"It's okay," Harvey said, his chest puffed. "I'm an adult and I'm paving my own path. She can't tell me what to do anymore."

I frowned. The hunters society didn't really think that way. Usually, the parents had control, or at least a heavy hand, on their kids' lives until they graduated the academy, which happened when they were twenty-one, twenty-two years old. But I was glad Harvey was sticking by my side. Rey would be proud of his friend.

Rey ...

A pang ran through my chest and I inhaled sharply. Every

time I thought of him, pain assaulted me, deep and unrelenting. Damn, how I wanted to drop everything and go after him.

I glanced at my mother. Although I wouldn't mind going after him right now, I knew my mother was right. When King Brikan revealed himself after the Shadow Trials a couple of days ago, he had tried to convince me to join him in the underworld. To become evil like him. When I refused, he spelled Rey and took him to the underworld.

According to my mother, Rey was too valuable to my father. He was bait for me. King Brikan wouldn't hurt Rey until I showed up. That didn't erase the unease and the urgency I felt. I wanted to go after Rey *right now*.

"What now?" Claire asked, her voice shy. Scared.

"First ..." My mother went around her desk and picked up something from underneath. I gasped, staring at the wooden box as she rested it on her desk. She opened it up and turned it to me. Inside, my Dawnblade greeted me. "Time to return this."

I closed my hands around my sword, feeling the magic inside. When Crimson had taken it from me a few weeks ago, I had felt like he had chopped off one of my limbs. "Thank you," I whispered.

"Second, we need to prepare the Demon Kissed Queens to fight King Brikan," she said, her voice solemn.

"Yeah, about that," Karen started. She crossed her arms and narrowed her eyes at my mother. "What does that entail, exactly? Because, you know, Kristin is only twelve. I hope you're not expecting her to march into the underworld and fight for real."

My mother let out a sigh. "I understand how you feel. Believe me, I tried keeping my daughter out of this life, but there are some things that are meant to happen. I'm sorry Kristin is only twelve, but I know she's here for a reason."

"That's not good enough! Our mother—"

"Karen, shut up!" Kristin snapped, startling all of us. The previous time I had met her, she had been so quiet and kind, seeing her explode like that was shocking. "Sorry." Her shoulders hunched. Now, I could see the girl I met before. "It's just … can't you see this is important? It's dangerous, but it's important too. I want to do this. Please."

"But …" Karen sighed.

"Let her do it," Katrina said. I had barely heard her speak before. "If you don't, she'll run off and do it anyway."

Kristin nodded. Karen's anguish was written all over her tense posture and the pinch in her nose. With another exasperated sigh, Karen retreated and sat on one of the chairs around the meeting table on the other side of the room.

Kristin stood tall. "How do we prepare to fight King Brikan?"

My mother's lips curled up for a brief moment, probably feeling proud of my little sister, but then she grew serious again. "I don't know, but I know who can tell us." She shifted her gaze to me. "I worked all winter break to find out where Fiona was hiding." So, that was why she was sneaking out of our apartment during winter break. "I finally found her a couple of days ago."

My jaw dropped. "You did? Where is she?"

"In Chasseur Ville," my mother said. She looked at all of us. "We're leaving to meet her in thirty minutes."

2

REY

THE SCENERY NEVER CHANGED IN THE UNDERWORLD. I HAD been locked in my suite atop one of the many turrets of the black palace for two days, and all I saw from the tall windows was the dark gray skies, the heavy clouds, the bright lightning, and below, the dark stone paths surrounded by an extensive lake of red lava.

I glanced down at myself. Atop my black shirt, a round red stone pendant hung from my neck. I ran my fingertips over it, the magic inside prickling my skin. King Brikan had forcefully put that over my head the moment I stepped inside his castle. It took away my magic, making me practically defenseless in a place full of demons. I couldn't even shift into my raven so I could fly away. Brikan had also taken my phone and smashed it to pieces in front of me.

At least the suite was comfortable. Brikan hadn't been kidding when he said he had luxurious guest rooms in his castle. My suite had a creepy vibe, with a black stone floor, black furniture, red bedding, black curtains, but everything was big, fancy, and each piece probably cost more than I would ever make per year as a professor at the academy.

I lay in the soft bed and closed my eyes.

Her face showed up instantly.

Erin.

Holy fuck, how I missed her. It had been only two days since her father had spelled me and lured me into the underworld, but I already missed her. And I worried about her. I worried because she was probably going crazy trying to think of how to rescue me.

Reyan, son of a prince of the underworld, ex-general to dozens of legions, and damsel in distress.

I let out a long sigh. But seriously, right about now, Erin had probably tried to escape from her mother's clutches about three hundred times, so she could charge into the underworld headfirst.

Fuck, I hoped Martha was able to keep a leash on her.

The doors opened and I didn't even pay attention to it. It was probably one of the demons, bringing me dinner. Or was it lunch next? It had only been two fucking days and I was already lost.

But then a shadow fell over me. I glanced to the side and saw a woman standing beside my bed. She smiled at me, revealing pearly white teeth, and her eyes blinked. A red shine covered them for a second.

A succubus.

She shifted her weight, throwing her hips to the side, and placed a hand on her waist, showing off her tightly wrapped red dress. "Hey, gorgeous. I'm Helia."

I groaned. "What is it?"

"Hm, in a bad mood? Aren't you yummy?" She reached to me with her sharp nails. I scooted away from her. "Though I would love to jump in that bed with you and give you a great time, King Brikan has asked for you." She flipped her long, red hair and took a step back. "Please, follow me."

I wanted to say no, but if I didn't go, I would just anger the Supreme Demon, and he could really show me what anger was.

I sighed and shot up from the bed. I followed the succubus out of my bedroom, past the two guards stationed at my door, down a dark hallway, down the wide stone stairs, through another long hallway, to a set of black double doors.

The succubus halted at the entrance and beckoned for me to walk past them. I stepped into a dark, round room and found King Brikan standing in the center, in human form, clad in a dark suit. Today, he was a tall man with long, black hair, and bright green eyes. Despite trying not to, I saw the resemblance between father and daughter. Was this his normal human form, or had he chosen this to irk me?

"Reyan, there you are," Brikan said with a fake smile. "How have the accommodations been? And the food? If you have any complaints, please let me know."

I frowned. "My complaint is being locked in."

"Ah." Brikan sighed. "I can't do anything about that. At least not yet."

I wouldn't take that bait or go down the rabbit hole. "Why did you summon me?"

"I gather you've been bored in your room." Brikan clasped his hands behind his back. "So, I thought you would like to start on the spell that will bring your mother and sister back."

I inhaled sharply. "You were serious."

"Of course I was. I might be a demon, Reyan, but a deal is a deal. I'll bring your mother and sister back."

I tried recalling our conversation. He had offered to bring

them back, and I had said yes, but that was just it. "It wasn't a deal."

His fake smile turned into sly grin. "Ah, I see you were paying attention. Good." Brikan unclasped his hands and brought his arms forward. A yellowed paper appeared, floating above his palm. "Like I told you before, the ceremony isn't easy and we need a powerful potion for it. The brewing of the ingredients will take a while, but honestly, I doubt Erin will rush into the underworld to save you in the next few days, so why not work on this?" He approached me and handed me the paper.

I didn't take it. "What is that?"

"This is a list of the ingredients we'll need." He shoved the paper against my chest. "You collect these from the castle grounds. Helia will help you." What he meant was that Helia would keep an eye on me. "Once you've gathered the first five items, return here. We can start brewing those."

I gripped the paper and looked at it. Scales of a baby dragon, wings of a living bat, mugwort, yarrow ... these were all dark items, and there were some here I had never heard of before. "This is the worst kind of dark magic."

Brikan chuckled. "What did you expect from a demon like me?" He raised his hand and shooed me off. "Go. Collect the items. Explore the castle. Pass the time. I'll see you back here later."

I stood my ground as Brikan turned his back to me.

If only I could use my magic, if only I could summon my Dawnblade, I could kill him right here, right now. Or so I wished. I doubted a simple hit of darkfire, or a stab to his heart would do the trick.

Helia appeared by my side and reached out her hand to me, her long, red nails clamping around my arm. "Let's go," she whispered. With a death grip, she pulled me out of the room. After closing the doors behind us, she turned to me. "What's the first ingredient on the list?"

My brows curled down. "I know you're not here to help me, but to keep an eye on me, so don't bother pretending."

She clicked her tongue. "Handsome and smart. Aren't you the complete deal? Alas, the sooner we get done with this, the sooner I can pass on babysitting duty."

I watched her, noting the magical traits that made this demon into a beautiful, almost irresistible woman. When a succubus attacked, human men couldn't fight it. They gave it all to her, even if they were madly in love with someone else. Because of my bloodline, her magic didn't work on me. I wondered ... if I had my magic and my Dawnblade, could I at least defeat her? I doubted Brikan had not-so-great demons working with him like this. But I liked to think I could have taken her down.

"Scales of a baby dragon," I told her. I also wanted to do this fast, but not to get rid of her, or because I wanted to get this spell done at once—though both were valid excuses. But because this would be an opportunity.

"That's at the apothecary," she said, marching down the hallway. "I bet you'll find most of the ingredients there."

I followed as she led me through the castle—and I worked on memorizing it, on noticing how many demons and guards were inside and stationed where, and searching for a clear exit. For about two hours, Helia and I went around the castle, gathering the first handful of ingredients, and from what I could see, the palace was full of demons of all kinds and ranks. Powerful guards were stationed in hallways and at the exits, which were few and heavily protected.

The little hope I had of finding a way of escaping died.

Until Helia took me to the top of the tallest turret, where we caught a live bat needed for the spell. We had encountered guards along the way, but there had been none beside the last door.

Pretending to look at the red and hot scenery outside, I leaned over the rail and glanced down. There were some tiles and decorations jutting out of the sides of the castle. It wouldn't be easy to scale down it, but this had been the only way out I had found so far. I knew for a fact that beyond the dark path disappearing under the black mountain in the horizon, just outside of Brikan's private estate, was one of the portals located in the underworld. I had used that one before.

"Careful, gorgeous," Helia said. "If you fall from up here, you'll certainly die."

Oh, I was sure of that, but I wasn't planning on falling. "No worries. I have no intentions of dying." I turned to her and eyed the passed-out bat in her hand. "Was that the last ingredient?"

"Of the first phase, yes. Let's go back to the king's chamber."

I nodded.

As I made my way back into the castle, I glanced over my shoulder, to the dark railing and the dark horizon. No, I had no intentions of dying, but I had every intention of escaping.

Tonight, when the demons thought I was sleeping, I would escape from the underworld.

3

IN THE END, NOT EVERYONE CAME WITH US TO CHASSEUR VILLE. It was just my mother, Claire, Harper, Ava, Tanner, and me. Harvey said he had something to do, Jasmin had no interest in participating of the preparation for the fight, just the actual fighting and later the looting, and Karen thought Kristin should stay out of everything she could. I knew that if she could, Karen would stop Kristin from fighting with us. If she did that, then everything would be in vain.

Although I hadn't the connection they had, and probably never would, Kristin was my sister too. Obviously, I didn't want her getting hurt, and I would do everything in my power to protect her. Karen could just ... chill a little.

Because of Brikan's attack, Chasseur Ville was practically closed. Blackthorn Hunters formed a barrier at the entrance of the town, not allowing tourists in. Thankfully, they knew my mother and had no problem letting us pass.

I glanced around, shocked to see the town so empty and quiet.

But my shock grew once my mother brought the SUV she

had taken from the academy into Francine's driveway—Harper's grandmother.

"Why are we here?" I asked my mother as we exited the car. "Does Francine know Fiona?"

Harper gasped. "No. She would have told us."

My mother opened her mouth to say something, but Francine beat her. "Hello, my dears." We turned toward her voice. She was standing in front of her open door, holding a tray with her delicious honey cookies. She smiled at us. "Come in."

Harper rushed in front of us. "Grandma, do you know Fiona?" she asked as she entered her grandmother's house. We stepped in right behind her.

Francine put the tray of cookies on the coffee table in the living room, then she faced her granddaughter. "My dear, I'm Fiona."

My eyes bugged, my muscles went rigid. "W-what?" I glanced from Francine to my mother. "Y-you knew?"

My mother shook her head. "Not until a few days ago." She pointed to Francine. "I came to her and she agreed to see you."

"As Fiona," Francine said. I shook my head. Holy shit, this was confusing. "Fiona was my name when I was a Wildthorn witch. I changed it when I joined the hunters. Only a handful of people knew the truth." She tilted her head, her eyes landing on each of us. "Well, more than a handful now." She gestured to the couch beside. "Come on, now. You know me. I won't bite."

My mother marched ahead and took a seat in one of the armchairs around the coffee table. Harper was the next one, dragging her feet until she was right beside her grandma. "I didn't know ..."

"Because I hadn't told you yet." Francine—or Fiona—pushed Harper down on the couch, then gestured for Claire, Ava, Tanner, and me to join her. The three-cushion couch was a little snug with the four of us sitting on it—Tanner sat on the couch's arm—but I was too worried about other things now.

"I looked everywhere for you," Tanner said, staring at Fiona with round eyes. "If only I had known you were so close."

My brows knitted together. "Why didn't you tell us before?"

"Because it wasn't important," she said, taking another one of the armchairs. What did she mean, it wasn't important? "First, you had to find your sisters. Now that you're together, I can tell you the prophecy, about the curse, and about the bond."

I jerked my head back. "W-what? Prophecy, curse, and bond? They are all the same thing?"

"No." Fiona shook her head. "They are all different. The Demon Kissed Queens prophecy, the Infernal Curse, and the Soul Bond."

The Soul Bond ... "What are you talking about?"

"Let's get to it," Fiona said, sounding younger and more energetic than I had ever seen her before. "I know you all want to know about the Demon Kissed Queens prophecy."

"Right," my mother said in my place. "That's why we came."

"Well, I can't tell you," Fiona said.

"Why not?" I asked, incredulous.

"Because ... you don't need to know about it yet. Besides, to make it really work, you and your sisters will have to come together, overcome your differences, and figure out what the prophecy means by yourselves. Otherwise, it'll be weak and it might not work."

What the hell did that mean? "But—"

"As for the Infernal Curse," she continued, not letting me finish. "That's the name of the spell you'll need to defeat King Brikan. Only once you and your sisters master using your magic together will you be ready to perform the curse and face the Supreme Demon."

"The Infernal Curse?" I asked. "I haven't heard of it."

"It's not common knowledge; otherwise, everyone would try to use it to defeat King Brikan, even though the spell is useless if not performed by the three Demon Kissed Queens." Fiona frowned. "No one is eating." She picked up the tray and passed it around. "Please, eat. I made them for you."

Everyone snatched a cookie or two from the tray, but nobody ate them.

"So, what is the Infernal Curse? How do we learn it?" I asked, playing with the cookie in my hand. This cookie was seriously delicious, but I was so worked up, I couldn't eat it.

"I'll teach you," Fiona said, resting the tray over the table once more. "We'll set up a day and time, and I'll teach it to you and your sisters."

"That would be a big help," my mother said, sounding relieved. "Thank you, Fiona."

"My pleasure." She zeroed her big eyes on me. "I know you came because of the prophecy and the curse, but I also know you wanted to ask me, Fiona, about something else. Go ahead. Ask me."

I gulped. How the hell did she know all that? I stole a glance at my mother, hoping she didn't get too mad at me about my question. "Hm, I want to rescue Rey, and I want to ask you if you can help me."

"There it is." She slapped her hands on her knees. "I can't help you enter the underworld and go after him, as you're imagining, but I can help you with the next best thing."

"Which is?"

"Remember the third one I mentioned when I started this conversation?" she asked. She lifted her index finger. "The Demon Kissed Queens prophecy." She lifted her middle finger. "The Infernal Curse." She lifted her ring finger. "The—"

"The Soul Bond," I said with a gasp. "What do you mean by that?"

"Only a powerful magical bond will be able to keep him sane enough and bring the two of you back together," she said. An invisible hand clutched at my heart. Keep him sane enough? What the hell did that mean? "That's the Soul Bond."

"But ... we destroyed it months ago."

She nodded. "There might be a way to restore the Soul Bond."

4

REY

IT HAD BEEN STUPID OF ME TO THINK THAT AT NIGHT I WOULD have a chance to escape. As it was, most demons never slept, and the palace was crawling with them just as much as during the day—not that I could discern time by looking at the view outside. I only knew what time it was when I looked at my wristwatch.

But at least, since we started brewing the first phase of the spell, King Brikan had told me I could walk freely around his castle. Although, freely meant either with Helia, or with two other demons trailing my every step. They would probably follow me to the fucking bathroom.

So, in the middle of the night, I pretended to have insomnia and a sudden need to walk around aimlessly. The two guards, ugly one and ugly two, followed me as I roamed the castle, looking for another escape route, and then, when I realized there was really no other way, to the top of the tallest turret.

The bats still flew low here. I waved my hand above my head, shooing them off as I made my way to the ledge of the tower. I leaned over the metal rail, looking at the ground, very distant from here.

Helia was right. If I fell, there was no way I would survive that. Better not to fall, then.

"Careful," ugly one snarled.

"I'm just looking," I said. With exaggerated movements, I stretched my arms wide, as if I was yawning, and leaned over some more.

Pretending to lose my balance, I yelped and fell out over the rails. I swiped at a stone jutting out the stone wall, and swung myself down to a tall window with a wider ledge.

Ugly one and ugly two yelped and rushed to the rail. They spied over the edge and yelled curses at me.

"I'll kill you!" ugly one roared before running away.

I was sure they were coming this way, going down the stairs, in the hopes to find me in the window. Which meant I had to move fast. I swung down to another stone detail, and then another, going slowly down. The muscles of my arms, shoulders, and back screamed at me. I might exercise a lot, but scaling a giant wall and relying a lot on my arms was new. If I didn't fall to my death, I would be so fucking sore after.

My escape didn't go unnoticed for long. Besides ugly one and ugly two, who had probably alerted half the castle about what I was doing, demons on the ground had spotted me. They shouted at me.

And then they threw darkfire at me.

"Fuck," I mumbled as I tried to go faster, to swing from ledge to ledge faster. I blocked my mind from thinking what I would do once I arrived on the ground. Confront all these demons? This plan had been rashly put together and rashly executed. All because I couldn't stand being here anymore.

I jumped to another window, but as my foot found

purchase on the wide stone ledge, a darkfire bolt grazed against my side, throwing me off-balance. I lost my grip on the stones.

And I fell.

Fear clutched my chest and all I could think about was that I would die and never see Erin again.

Though I could barely breathe with the despair raging inside of me, I closed my eyes and accepted my fate.

I suddenly stopped.

I opened my eyes and found myself floating in midair. From one of the lower castle balconies, Brikan stood, his hand extended toward me. He closed his hand and pulled his arm back. Like a feather whirling in the wind, I swam in the air until I was standing right in front of him. Brikan put me down. My knees buckled with the sudden drop and I almost fell at his feet. I stumbled back, gaining some distance from the king of the underworld.

Brikan's eyes darkened. "Oh, Reyan." He tsked. "I've got to say, I'm rather disappointed, because I thought you were smarter than this." His lips stretched into a wicked grin. "But ... I'm pleased. Now I can stop playing kind host and get to the fun part."

Red clasps appeared around my wrists, joining them in front of me. "What the fuck?"

Without a word, Brikan started walking. The red clasps tugged me forward, and without a choice, I followed him, almost tripping on my feet to keep up.

Demon guards fell into step behind us, though I was sure Brikan didn't need reinforcements against me. What else could I do? I couldn't use my fucking magic or my Dawnblade, and now I was chained.

Fuck. In my haste to get away from here, I had overlooked

many of the risks, thinking, wishing, hoping I could escape them. For some reason, I hadn't expected demons to be waiting for me on the ground. In my mind, I just jumped down and ran to the portal. But that had been so fucking stupid of me. I had played with fire, and now I would get burned.

As I expected, Brikan took me to the dungeons, but this one wasn't like the dungeons at the Blackthorn Hunters Academy. No, Brikan's looked like a specialized business. Like the rest of the castle, the walls and floors were dark, but the stones were polished, the torture chairs and pillars all smooth and clean, the chains new, the tools spread across the glass tables were shiny.

The red clasps pulled me until I was standing between two stone pillars that reached up to the tall ceiling. The clasps separated and brought my arms up above my head. Then, metal chains shot down from the pillars, tying around my wrists. More chains appeared from below, wrapping around my ankles and keeping my legs apart.

"Hello, Reyan," a new voice said.

I watched as Coyne strolled into the dungeon. His dark eyes fixed on mine, a knowing glint in them. Last time I had seen him, Coyne, who had been a famous demon hunter and a professor this past semester, had stood up to Crimson at the end of the Shadow Trials, and stopped the whole thing. Then he attacked, revealing he was one of King Brikan's lackeys.

I narrowed my eyes at him. "So, what are you? A shapeshifter?"

"No, I simply possessed this body," he said, as if it was the most normal thing to have a demon possessing humans. Well, maybe in the demon hunter world it was, but it still didn't make it right.

King Brikan turned to Coyne. "Would you like to have a turn?"

Coyne shook his head. "I won't spoil your fun."

"Good." With the wicked grin stamped on his face, Brikan halted before me. "Won't you beg?"

I snorted. "What good will that do? I bet that if I beg, my torture will be even worse."

Brikan nodded. "At least you understand how the game works." He walked to the nearest table and picked up a thick leather whip. "Let's start with something simple."

This was going to be one fucking long night.

5

———

ERIN

I stared at Fiona, sure I hadn't heard her right. "You're saying ..."

She nodded. "You might be able to restore the Soul Bond."

"But how is this possible?" Claire asked. "She and Rey severed it. They let out a demon and almost died."

"Right," I said, trying to think through this craziness. "The bond is gone."

Fiona pressed her lips into a thin line. "Yes and no. The Soul Bond is a onetime thing. Meaning you'll never be able to bond with anyone else. You might be able to break it, but the *why behind* the bond, the connection the twin souls shared, it's still there. You might not have the mark on your chest anymore, or feel the connection, but you can't just erase such a powerful bond, not totally."

I blinked, still trying to process what she was saying. "So, you mean Rey and I are still soulmates?" Fiona nodded. This was unexpected, but good. I liked the idea of being connected to Rey again. "All right … so, if I were to restore the bond, what do I have to do?"

"You'll need to summon a more powerful being," Fiona said. "An angel this time. You need to convince the angel that you're doing this for the right reason, and not selfish ones. You need to prove it."

"That should be easy," I said. Nothing was more right than my love for Rey.

Fiona shook her head. "I haven't heard of many people trying to restore a Soul Bond before, but the ones that I heard about, failed. It has never been done before."

"Well, it shouldn't be too bad, right?" Ava asked, eyeing us. "If she fails, then we go to plan B."

"Wait." My mother raised a hand. "What happens if she fails?"

Fiona hesitated. "Then the angel will take her life."

"Oh, never mind," Ava muttered.

"This is too risky," Harper protested.

"I agree," Claire said. "We can't lose you."

Tanner tsked, shaking his head.

"That's it, then," my mother said, slapping her knees. "We forget about restoring the Soul Bond, and move on to learning the Infernal Curse. How does—?"

"No," I started. They all stared at me. "I want to do it. I'll do anything to help bring Rey back. I don't care about the risks, because I'm sure it's going to work." Deep in my heart, I had always considered Rey my soulmate, with or without a bond to connect us. We had been made for each other. Confident, I fixed my gaze on Fiona. "What do I have to do?"

"You need to go into isolation for a few hours, perform a cleansing ritual, and meditate, thinking about what you'll say to the angel. Then, at the same place you severed the bond, you summon the angel and ask him to restore it."

I frowned. "Just like that?"

"Just like that."

It seemed simple enough, but nothing so far had been simple. Everything turned out to be way more complicated. This too wasn't going to be easy, I was sure.

But it didn't matter.

For Rey, I would do anything.

***

AFTER FIONA'S INSTRUCTIONS, MY MOTHER TOOK US BACK TO the academy. On the way, she tried to convince me that I was being stupid for trying to restore the bond.

"We'll figure some other way of helping him," she said, her voice laced with concern. Claire, Harper, and Ava joined her, saying it was too risky. I had to think of the bigger goal. If I died trying to restore the bond and failed, then Brikan would never be defeated.

I reminded them that someone else would show up with the mark after me, like before there was Cindy and Brianne. There would always be someone. They just had to look for it.

"Erin, please, this is ridiculous," my mother continued.

I shut them down right there and then. "Nothing you say will convince me not to perform the ceremony."

When we got to the academy, I told them I would do the cleansing the ritual right away. They should get ready because once I was back, we would perform the ceremony.

I thought my mother would argue with me some more, or maybe even hold on to me so I couldn't go, but she stared at me, her eyes saying more than her words.

It didn't matter. I wasn't going to change my mind.

So, with Rey in my mind and heart, I went to the forest, my boots crunching on the dried grass, recently emerged from underneath the snow. The wind whipped at my hair, still too chilly for my taste, ruffling the leafless branches of the trees.

At what I thought Fiona would think was a nice spot, I cleared some of the snow that still hadn't melted away, spread the crystals Fiona had lent to me in a small circle, and sat in the center on the hard grass, my legs crisscrossed.

Following Fiona's instructions, I inhaled deeply and cleared my mind. Instantly, the crystals hummed. They were active. The ritual was on.

And I was one step closer to rescuing Rey.

6

THE MAGIC HOLDING THE CHAINS UP BROKE AND I FELL TO MY knees on the hard, cold floor.

"Enough for now," Brikan said, wiping his hands on a black towel.

Coyne stood beside me, wrinkling his nose. "All that blood, it really accents your pale complexion." He chuckled, a sick sound that grated at my ears.

"Take him to his room," Brikan barked.

Guards ugly one and ugly two hooked their hands under my arms and hoisted me up. They carried me to my bedroom, where they threw me at the bed, even though my shirt was ripped to pieces and blood was seeping from the wounds on my back, staining the bedsheets.

Without a word, they left.

Alone, I inhaled deeply, but that only made the cuts on my back hurt more. I groaned as the pain rippled through my body. Brikan had whipped my back over twenty times—I had stopped counting then, because knowing how many there were only made me more desperate.

It was all my fucking fault. I deserved it for not planning more.

It wouldn't happen again. Next time I acted, I was going to make it.

But for now, I had to rest.

Right when I thought I was falling asleep, a demon with curling horns behind his bald head entered the bedroom. Holding a black bag, he approached my bed.

"I'm Ixon, a healer."

I snorted. "After skinning me alive, Brikan sent a healer to fix me up?"

Ixon shook his head. "I'm not here to fix you up. I was just sent to make sure you don't die."

Of course. Brikan needed me alive if he wanted Erin to come rescue me.

Holy shit, Erin. If she knew about my half-assed attempt at an escape, she would beat me up too.

Even though he wasn't supposed to heal me, I saw as the demon healer cleaned my wounds and applied some kind of paste on them. It burned on contact, but it soon became a chill that numbed the pain. Then, he bandaged the worst ones.

"You should drink lots of water and rest for a while," the healer said right before exiting my bedroom.

Right now, I didn't want anything. No water, no food. I just wanted to make the pain go away and to sleep.

Drained, it didn't take long for the darkness to carry me.

I DIDN'T KNOW HOW LONG I SLEPT, BUT WHEN I WOKE UP, THERE was a tray of food beside the bed—French toast, bacon, eggs, and coffee. Breakfast, so I was assuming it was morning. Or at least, it had been.

Slowly, I sat up in bed, groaning as pain ricocheted across my back. I forced myself to stand and go to the bathroom, where I stripped off my ripped shirt, and took off the bandages the healer had applied over my wounds.

To my surprised, the long lines across my back were thin and white, as if they were ten years old. The healer said he wouldn't heal me, but that was exactly what he did. Otherwise, how could my wounds have become like this overnight?

Holding my breath, I rolled my shoulders. Despite the pain when I first got out of the bed, now my back felt sore.

After taking a quick shower and putting on clean clothes, I sat down with my breakfast, but before I could eat, I found a note beside the coffee cup.

I read it.

You're free to roam the castle again. Try something like that again, and I'll make sure you can't recover next time.

When you can, meet me in the potions chamber.

There was no signature, but it was obvious it was from Brikan.

I ate my breakfast and went to the potions chamber—followed by ugly one and ugly two.

When I got there, a demon knelt in front of Brikan, and Coyne stood a few steps back. I paused at the entrance, feeling like I shouldn't be here.

"You ..." Brikan groaned. "I'm surrounded by incompetent demons. That's the only explanation."

"I'm sorry, my king," the demon uttered, his voice trembling. "I promise it'll never happen again."

"I've heard that before." Brikan raised his hands and let them fall.

An invisible knife cut across the demon's skull, severing his body in two. The two pieces fell to the ground, blood spreading wide in a shallow pool.

My stomach turned with the sight.

Brikan snapped his fingers and it was all gone. The body, the blood, the mess.

I stared at him, both in awe and fear. Here was the devil in the flesh. The worst soul ever to exist. And the most powerful. I couldn't play around with Brikan. I had to be more careful.

"Reyan is here, my king," ugly one announced.

Brikan raised his eyes to me and showed me one of his wide, fake smiles. "I see you're feeling better."

Coyne snorted. "You should have gone for his face."

Ignoring the other demon, Brikan tilted his head, appraising me. "What I did yesterday was just a small punishment, Reyan. If you don't behave, things can go south. Yes, I need you alive if I want Erin to come to me, that's no secret, but I'm very powerful, you know." He leaned forward and lowered his voice, as if he was telling me a secret. "I can kill you and then do a spell so she believes you're still alive." He gestured to Coyne. "Or I can have a demon possess your body. Simple."

Coyne licked his lips, clearly eager for that option.

Fuck.

Inhaling deeply, I walked closer. "Did you want to see me?" It killed me to ask him this, as if I was one of the thousands of demons who worked for him, who cowered at the mention of his name.

"I did." He gestured to the table behind him, crammed full of vials, tubes, bowls, and equipment. "Despite everything, I'm not a liar, Reyan. The potion for the spell is almost ready."

I frowned. "You said it would take a long time."

He shrugged. "I might have infused some of my magic in it to speed up the process." He walked around the table and gestured to something there.

I followed him and saw a stone box, much like a small tomb. Inside were several, if not hundreds, of gray bones.

"What is this?" I asked, dreading the answer.

"Your mother's and sister's bones." He looked at me, his dark eyes twinkling. "Tomorrow, we'll perform the spell and bring them back."

7

ERIN

EARLY THE NEXT MORNING, FIONA CAME TO THE ACADEMY AND we met in the courtyard, where the Blackthorn tree was located. Even though it wasn't required, everyone had come to support me—Claire, Harper, Ava, Harvey, Jasmin, Kristin, Karen, and Katrina. The only one who was here but was clearly against this was my mother.

Again, she tried to talk me out of the ceremony.

"Erin, please, listen to me," she said again. "I'll find another way to protect Rey, to find him, to bring him back, whatever. Just … don't do this. It's too risky."

Under the tree, I turned to her. "Mom, I'll say this one more time. Stop or I'll ask Fiona to cast a spell on you to either keep you back or freeze you until this is done. Or you stay quiet and watch, like the others. It's your choice."

My mother glanced at Fiona, who was standing a few feet behind me, her eyes begging. But Fiona didn't relent. She knew I had to do this and nothing would change my mind.

"I don't want to spell you, Martha," Fiona said, serious. "Please stand back."

My mother let out a long sigh and retreated to where my friends were—on the front steps of the Statice building, where they could see it all, but from a safe distance.

Fiona rested a hand on my shoulder. "Are you ready?"

I exhaled deeply. "I am."

Fiona squeezed my shoulder before letting it go. She took a few steps back and faced the tree. She opened her hands wide and began chanting in a language I didn't understand.

A moment later, the air vibrated, the ground trembled. An explosion of light blinded me for an instant. When I was able to open my eyes again, an angel hovered in midair.

A beautiful female angel with long, blond hair, silky skin. She wore a white gown, a thin golden tiara around her forehead, and had wide, graceful white wings. Light seemed to emanate from every pore and every feather. A sense of calm and righteousness fell over me.

The angel looked down at me with bright blue eyes. "Who dares to summon me?" Her voice was strong and gentle at the same time.

I puffed out my chest. "I did."

"What for?"

"I have a request. Please, restore the Soul Bond I used to share with Rey Lowe."

"Reyan, son of Prince Asmodeus, and Erin, daughter of King Brikan. Twin souls. Soulmates indeed." She appraised me. "How will you convince me to grant your request?"

"By telling you that Reyan was taken by King Brikan to serve as a bait for me. He was taken because of me. And as his twin soul, his soulmate, I wish to save him. Having the Soul Bond restored will help me connect with him in order to help him."

"That isn't enough," she announced, her tone harsher

than before. "I believe you're trying to restore the bond because it's too painful to live without him, and you just want him back to make you happy. Therefore, it's a selfish wish."

"No! That's not true!" I shouted.

The angel whirled her hand and a long, silver sword appeared in her grip. "Prepare to die."

The angel raised the sword high. Screams reached my ears, but I shut them out.

I had done this. I had risked my life to save Rey. If given the chance, I would do it again.

I lowered my head, accepting my fate. But before I died, I whispered, "I don't care if I die. Right now, all I want is to save Rey. Even if I die, I need to make sure he gets home safely."

I waited for the sword to drop, my stomach tense, my mind reeling, a little afraid of feeling any pain.

But it never came.

When I dared look up, the angel was right in front of me. She had put the sword away and her feet were on the ground. "Now, that is selfless," she said with a faint smile. "You care about Reyan more than you care about yourself, as you're willing to give your life for his. That's the real meaning of being a soulmate. No one else who performed the ceremony before was willing to do so." She paused. "The Soul Bond becomes stronger than before because of it." She pressed a hand on my chest. "I give you the Soul Bond back."

A jolt of pure electricity and magic and pain coursed through me, bringing me to my knees. I screamed as the pain intensified, until it robbed me of all air. I swayed to the side, dizzy and numb.

"Erin!" someone shouted.

Hands clasped my shoulders and helped me up. I leaned against someone.

"Are you okay?" my mother asked. I spied through my lashes. She was hovering over me, her hands ready to catch me.

Opening my eyes some more, I looked down at myself. I lowered the neck of my shirt and stared at the dark mark right above my left breast.

The Soul Bond.

8

A SHARP PAIN ON MY CHEST WOKE ME UP. I SAT UP IN MY BED, gasping for air as the pain coursed through my body, slowly fading away. I rubbed at my chest, where the pain had started, confused. In my daze, I spied under my shirt.

The Soul Bond mark was back.

I jumped from the bed and ran to the bathroom, where I took off my shirt and examined myself in the mirror. Yes, it was the fucking Soul Bond, imprinted just an inch above my heart, like before.

How could this be possible? Erin and I had destroyed the Soul Bond, and as far as I knew, the twin soul thing was a once in a lifetime deal. I wouldn't find another soulmate, because even though the bond had been destroyed, Erin was and would always be my only soulmate.

Then, what the fuck did this mean? That our Soul Bond had simply come back? It didn't make sense.

But ... I chose to believe. I chose to hold on to this. If the bond had come back, then it had to mean something. Not just that Erin was my one and only, but that we would be reunited again. That we would succeed.

A little excited about this new development, I didn't go back to sleep. Instead, I exercised, keeping my body ready if I needed to fight my way out or use my strength to scale down another wall—not that I would try that anytime soon.

When Helia came in my room early in the morning, she was surprised to find me up. "What's up with you?" she asked, as I ran a towel through my damp hair. I had already showered and dressed, ready for whatever this fucking day would bring.

I quickly ate the breakfast Helia had brought to me, then followed her to the potions chamber.

Again, she stopped at the door and gestured for me to go inside alone. Usually, this had brought me dread, but not today. Today, I was ready for whatever the world brought on.

Fuck, I was so wrong.

Brikan stood in front of a shallow pool of clear water that had mysteriously showed up in the center of the room overnight. Coyne was nowhere to be seen.

"Oh, you're just in time," Brikan said as I approached him.

My brow furrowed. "In time for what?"

He showed me a wicked smile. "For the awakening."

The Supreme Demon threw my mother's and my sister's bones in the pool, then dumped a flask with the potion we had been working on with it. He offered another small flask with the same potion on it. "Drink this."

I eyed the flask. "Why?"

"It's part of the ritual," Brikan said, his tone firm. "This is what connects you to them."

I didn't like this, but I knew that if I didn't drink it by

myself, Brikan would either force it down my throat, or he would stop the ceremony. I didn't want any of that to happen.

Wrinkling my nose, I drank the fucking potion, gagging at its foul taste. I expected to feel sick, or weird, but other than the brief awful taste, nothing happened. At least to me.

Not five seconds later, the water started bubbling and boiling, turning red. When the bubbles were gone, two figures emerged from the water, floating like ghosts.

My heart seized in my chest.

Stunned, I watched as Brikan moved his hands, and my mother and my sister glided above water, to the edge of the pool. They stepped onto the stone ground and halted right in front of me.

Breathing hard, I blinked, not believing my eyes. It couldn't be. It had worked. Holy fuck, it had worked.

Vision blurred by hot tears, I embraced them.

But they didn't move. They didn't touch me, they didn't turn to me, they didn't even blink. They stood there, staring ahead like lifeless dolls.

I turned to Brikan. "What the fuck is this?"

Brikan shrugged. "I said I could bring them back, I didn't say how."

What the ...? Rage coiled in my core. I clenched my fists, trying to contain it, but I couldn't. After all he had done to me —robbing me of Erin, using me as bait to catch her, torturing me, and now tricking me with the lives of my mother and sister—I couldn't contain it.

My rage exploded, heating up my blood.

I marched to him and grabbed the collar of his shirt. "What did you do?"

Brikan let out a hollow chuckle. "I've brought back their bodies, but I can't do much about their souls."

I dropped my hands from him, shocked. What the fuck had he done? "So ..." I glanced over my shoulder, to the bodies of my mother and sister. "They aren't alive."

Brikan smoothed out the collar of his shirt. "Not in the same sense you are."

My rage came back in full force. I punched him in the jaw.

Brikan's head snapped to the side. I was ready to go again, but he raised his hand and magic wrapped around me, making me still. I fought against his power, but it was in vain. I couldn't win against him, not like this.

"I'll kill you," I shouted, because it was all I could do.

"Right." Brikan ran a hand over his jaw, as if checking if it was all right. Though the punch had brought me brief satisfaction, I knew I couldn't really hurt him. He was checking himself for show. "I was going to leave them like this for your sake, but since you're misbehaving again ..."

Brikan waved my mother and sister off.

Like obedient robots, they turned around and stepped into the pool. They went down, as if the pool was several feet deep.

They were gone.

A sob rose to my throat but I swallowed it. I wouldn't cry in front of him.

Brikan turned his devil eyes to me and his lips stretched in his trademark wicked grin. "Now, we'll play again."

ERIN

In my combat training uniform, I sat down on the mat and stretched. I had no idea what Fiona had planned for us, but I was pumped.

And it was all because of the Soul Bond.

Yesterday, we had restored it, but last night, I had felt Rey. I was sure of it. This hadn't happened the first time we had the Soul Bond, but maybe now it was different, not because it had been restored, but because it had evolved. At least, that was what I wanted to believe.

Either way, I had felt him, like a tug in my chest. And I was sure that if I followed that tug, it would take me to him.

Ready to storm the underworld and rescue my man, I got dressed and ready, and went to my mother's office in the Aster building. I told her about the feeling, but she dismissed me, saying that going into the underworld without mastering the Infernal Curse was suicide. We argued, but in the end, she convinced me. I knew she was right, but it was freaking hard to sit here and wait.

And that was how I ended up in the Hyacinth building to

train. I came early, stretched, then workout by myself by lifting weights, doing fighting drills, and sword play.

By the time Fiona arrived, I had already been in the building for almost two hours.

"Do you need a break?" she asked as she walked in. Her hair was tied in a low bun at the base of her head, and she wore a long cloak that gave her a mystical air.

My brain was still having problems thinking about her as Francine *and* Fiona, the gentle grandma who baked comfort cookies and the powerful witch who could tell prophecies.

I shook my head. "Nope. Let's keep going."

"If you say so," she muttered.

In no time, Jasmin and Kristin arrived, flanked by Karen and Katrina. Although Fiona had warned the others the training was just for the three Demon Kissed Queens, Karen and Katrina had come along with their youngest sister. But Fiona was adamant. She wouldn't start the training session until Karen and Katrina left, even if all they did was stand behind the closed door.

So that was what they did.

And Fiona started.

She faced the three of us, her face kind and relaxed. "To enact the Infernal Curse, you will need to unite your power as one. The three of you will have to become one."

Jasmin frowned. "And what the hell does that mean?"

I glanced at her. I knew my mother had gave her, and also Kristin, the same combat training uniform I wore, but apparently, she didn't do uniforms. She decided to wear red leather leggings, high-heeled boots, and a skin-tight black sweater, along with several bracelets, necklaces, and long earrings. It seemed like she was going to a party, and not to learn how to defeat the devil himself.

"It means you'll have to be tolerant and understanding," Fiona went on. "And you'll have to work as one." Jasmin rolled her eyes, and Kristin rolled her shoulders. At least the youngest of us seemed eager to help. Fiona went on. "Can all of you conjure darkfire?"

I raised my hand in front of me and summon a bolt of darkfire in my open palm. Jasmin did the same, though she purposely made her bolt bigger than mine.

Kristin brought her hand up. She frowned, focusing on her magic, but just a spark appeared in her palm before fading away. "I've never done it," she confessed, her voice low.

Holy shit. I didn't want to be disappointed in the girl, but not knowing how to even conjure her power set us back.

"It's okay." Fiona walked to her. She held Kristin's hand in hers. "I'll help you. Just think of your power and imagine the darkfire appearing in your hand, just like Erin and Jasmin did. I'll guide you."

Kristin took a long breath and tried again. With Fiona's help, the darkfire shone bright in her hand. The young girl grinned. "I did it!"

Jasmin tsked. "With Fiona's help."

"It's okay," Fiona said. "I helped you, yes, but now you know how it's supposed to be, how it's supposed to feel. You'll be able to do it alone now." She stepped back, letting go of Kristin's hands. "Try again."

A knot appeared in Kristin's brow as she focused and tried to conjure her darkfire. I thought she wouldn't be able to do it, but after a few seconds, a spark appeared in her hand, and it slowly grew into a perfect bolt of darkfire.

"I did it!" she cried, smiling wide.

"Good job," I said, matching her smile.

"Great. Now we can continue," Fiona said, drawing our

attention back to her. "Conjure your darkfire." We did. Fiona pulled a tall, heavy bag from the side and placed it across the room. "Aim it here." She tapped the center of the standing bag. "But before you throw it, unite your darkfire."

The bolt flickered in my hand. "How?"

"Meet in the middle," Fiona said, as if that made sense. "As you throw it, think about uniting it along the way, converging all that power together. The bolts should start as three, but find their target as one."

"It shouldn't be hard," Jasmin said, her voice flat. She was already bored. "Let's just do it."

Fiona pressed her lips together. "All right. Are you ready?" We nodded. "On three, throw the bolts." She stepped to the side, giving us space. "One. Two. *Three!*"

We threw our darkfire to the target. Jasmin's and mine hit the target, though they didn't converge together. In fact, mine hit the target before hers. As for Kristin's ... the girl wasn't used to aiming and hitting her target. She missed it by a few feet, hitting the wall on the back and leaving a black burn on the white paint.

"I'm not good at this," Kristin said, her voice trembling.

"Obviously!" Jasmin snapped. "How do you plan on fighting the king of the underworld if you can't even hit a goddamn target?"

"Hey!" I called out. "She's never done this. Give her a break."

"A break?" Jasmine glared at me. "I want to get this over with, if you haven't noticed."

Oh, I had noticed, and I was in the same boat. The sooner we got this done, the better. But not long ago, I had been new to all of this, and I had been older than Kristin. She was thirteen and so much depended on her. It was too freaking much.

"She'll get it," I replied, stepping closer to Kristin. I felt like embracing her to give her strength, but I wasn't sure if that would help, or make her feel worse. "We just need to practice a little more."

Jasmin threw up her hands. "This is ridiculous. We'll never be able to defeat the Supreme Demon, and it'll be all because of her." She jerked her chin toward Kristin.

Tears rolled down Kristin's face.

"Jasmin, that's enough!" Fiona interjected, her voice firm.

The door opened and Karen and Katrina stepped in. Once they saw Kristin crying, they acted. Katrina ran to Kristin, and Karen turned to Jasmin and me.

"What did you do?" she barked, in total mama bear mode.

"She'll be okay—"

"She's weak and can't do it," Jasmin said, interrupting me. "The way it's going, she'll be the first to die when we face our father."

"Jasmin!" I cried, shocked by her lack of manners.

"I said that's enough!" A ripple of magic ran through the room and we all turned to Fiona. "Karen, Katrina, everything is okay. The training will be hard, and the girls will be stressed every once in a while. Kristin, we'll practice more and I'm sure you'll be as good as the others in no time. Jasmin, you're out of line. Behave or I'll be the one facing you."

Jasmin snorted. "I didn't sign up for this." She stomped out of the practice room and slammed the door behind her back.

"Damn it." Kristin sniffed. "We need Jasmin, but now she's mad because of me."

"Don't worry, my dear," Fiona said. "She'll come around, you'll see."

I turned to Fiona. "What about if I practice with Kristin?" While Jasmin cooled off, we could train and get her up and running. "We can take a quick break now to regroup, and then I can start her on small, simple spells so she can learn to call her magic and use it."

Fiona nodded. "That sounds like a good idea." She let out a long sigh. "And I'll go talk to Jasmin." She patted Kristin's shoulder. "Don't worry, my dear. You'll get it and everything will be okay." She turned her eyes to me. "Meet me here tomorrow morning, at the same time."

I nodded.

Fiona acknowledged Karen and Katrina before leaving the room and going after Jasmin. Good luck to her.

I offered Kristin a soft smile. "How about we go get a snack before we continue training."

The young girl wiped her tears from her eyes and nodded at me.

THAT NIGHT, IT TOOK ME A LONG TIME TO FALL ASLEEP. FIRST because, even though I was tired from training all day, I was also sore and a little anxious about where we were going. I practiced with Kristin for hours, until the little girl couldn't take anymore. But by the end of the day, she was able to hit her target ninety percent of the time. She still had a lot to learn and improve, but at least now Fiona would be able to continue with her lesson, and we would learn more about the Infernal Curse.

Second, because I couldn't stop dreaming about the Shadow Trials and how Rey had become a robot in Brikan's hand. He had attacked me and he had been lured into the underworld, taken by my father as bait. In my dreams, I stood in the center of the arena, either fighting him or running from demons Brikan had unleashed on me.

But then the dream changed. The demons were gone and I was alone in the arena.

Until Rey stepped into my line of sight.

"Erin?" he called, unsure.

I narrowed my eyes at him. "Stay back, or I'll kick your ass."

He raised both his hands in a peace gesture. "I'm not under his control now." He looked around, then his eyes fixed on mine again. "I think this is a dream."

I nodded. "This is my dream."

"No, this is my dream."

I gasped. "Could ..."

Rey's gray eyes widened. "You mean ... this isn't a dream?"

My heart accelerated and I dared taking a step closer. But Rey didn't hold back. He ran to me and wrapped his arms around me, pulling me tight against him. He buried his face in my neck and whispered, "This is not a dream."

I snaked my arms around his shoulders and clutched him, not willing to ever let go. "But how?"

He pulled back and locked those bright gray eyes on mine. "The Soul Bond. How—?"

"I restored it," I said, feeling immensely proud of it.

"How?"

"Fiona helped me."

"Wait. You found Fiona?"

I nodded. "I did, and I have Jasmin and Kristin with me. Things aren't going as smoothly as I would like, but we're training to take down Brikan."

A deep frown appeared between his brows. "Erin, he's too

strong. Please, don't rush in here if you're not one hundred percent ready."

I ran my hands around his shoulders. "Don't worry. We'll be ready, and I'll rescue you." I slid my hand down his back. "Wait. What's this?" I stepped out of his embrace and lifted his shirt, spying his back. There were several thin white lines across his skin. "What happened?"

Rey turned, pulling down his shirt. "Well ... I haven't been exactly quiet. I tried to escape, and last night, I punched your father."

My stomach dropped. "Wait, but I thought ... I thought he wouldn't hurt you because you're my bait."

Rey chuckled, a hollow sound. "Yeah, well, he won't kill me, but I don't think he'll stop torturing me." I clenched my fists, suddenly angry about this. When I faced Brikan, I wouldn't just kill him. I would make him suffer. Rey stepped into me and clutched my shoulder. "Forget about this. Just focus on learning the curse and defeating Brikan. I'll be okay." I shook my head, not liking how okay he would be. Rey cupped my face. "Erin, it's okay. I'm just glad about this. About seeing you, really you, not just a dream."

I leaned into his touch. "I'm guessing this is one of the perks of this renewed and stronger Soul Bond."

He showed me a lopsided smile and my heart skipped a beat. "I like it."

"Me too." I clutched his shirt and tugged him closer to me.

Rey leaned into me and lowered his face to mine, but before his lips touched mine, I woke up.

Breathing hard, I sat up in my bed. I glanced around, taken aback by the sudden change. One second, I was almost kissing Rey, and the next I was in my dark room, alone and lost.

Although I wished I could have held him for longer, a renewed sense of purpose washed over me. Even if I had to forgo sleep and train twenty-four-seven, I was going to master that damn Infernal Curse, invade the underworld, and kill the Supreme Demon.

And then Rey would be by my side again.

10

SEEING AND HOLDING ERIN IN MY DREAMS WAS LIKE BREATHING fresh air. Although he had tortured me twice, he kept trying to make me explode again, and his preferred method was to taunt me about the failed spell to bring back my mother and sister.

To make things worse, Coyne kept showing up unexpectedly, trying to rile me up. Thankfully, he was nowhere to be seen this morning.

"We should try it again," Brikan said with a grin. "Perhaps this time I can steal their souls from paradise."

I didn't even listen to his nonsense anymore. It wasn't worth my time. What I wanted to use my time for was to find a way of escaping. I had failed badly before, but I refused to believe this place was unbreakable.

But the problem was how? I kept on my walks around the castle, followed by ugly one and ugly two, trying to spot a place with less guards, less security, from where I could sneak through, and all I found was more of the same: this place was impossible to escape.

One morning, when I stepped out of my room, I was surprised to see a female demon standing in the place of ugly one and two. She wore thick, black armor with a helmet that covered everything but her eyes. While she followed me through the castle's hallways, I tried sensing what kind of demon she was, but she was either above my rank, or she was one of those kinds that were meant to confuse others. Either way, this was the first time I had one guard trailing my every move. I didn't have my magic or my sword, but I wondered if I could take her with my fighting skills alone.

The opportunity present itself when I entered the library —even the devil had a library in his castle—and found there was no one nearby.

In the center of the library, I turned to her and threw my hand to her, intent on striking her in the neck, where her helmet ended.

But she stepped back and raised a hand. "Rey, wait."

I stopped dead in my tracks. "Who the fuck are you?" The female took off the helmet. Her face looked odd, but after a while, the glamour was gone and I saw her. "Norah!" I almost smiled at her. Norah was a demon hunter in the Blackthorn Hunters main unit, and she had helped Erin and me a couple of times before. "What are you doing here?"

"Martha sent me to get you out," she said. "I infiltrated the underworld the same day you were taken, and thankfully, the spells she gave me are strong. I was able to pretend I was one of them, and last night, I switched the guards' schedule so I could be the one following you around. I planned on revealing myself once we were alone, but you attacked me first!"

"Sorry about that." I ran a hand through my hair. "But ... what now?"

"I've got a plan for us to get out of here, but you need to do exactly what I say." She fished a small tube from one of her pockets. "Here. Drink this."

I grabbed the vial with a thick clear liquid. "What's this?"

"Vampire venom," she explained. If humans drank this, it would either turn or kill them. But because I was half-demon, the venom would give me supernatural strength and speed, like a vampire.

Without hesitating, I drank the venom. It burned my throat and I gagged on the last drop, but thankfully, it stayed down. A moment later, I felt it. The power filling my veins, igniting my core. Demon hunters were inherently faster, stronger, and more agile than humans, but that was nothing compared to a vampire. We would soon see how this temporary-vampire-like-me fared against higher demons.

"So, what's the plan?" I asked, trying to get used to the new feeling inside me.

She smirked. "Come with me." Frowning, I followed her out of the library, through the hallways, to the front door of the castle. Because she was dressed up as a guard, nobody stopped us.

In front of the huge doors, Norah turned to me. "Brace yourself."

"For what?"

She didn't say it twice. With swift movements, Norah summoned her Dawnblade and jutted it at me. I gasped, sure she was stabbing me in the chest. But instead, a quick glass-breaking sound reached my ears. Jaw open in shock, I glanced down at my chest and saw the necklace.

Broken.

"You should be able to take it off now," she said, hiding

her sword once again. "But by now, Brikan probably knows something is going on." She rolled her shoulders. "Ready?"

I eyed her, confused. "What for?"

"Once we step through this door, we'll need to run faster than we've ever run before," she said. "That's why I gave you the vampire blood. Demons will come at us, and we'll fight them off, but we won't stop. You got it?"

I blinked. "That's your fucking plan?"

"You've got a better one?"

Actually, I didn't. "Fuck," I whispered.

She pushed the doors open, and we darted out, as a roar echoed inside the castle. The shuffle of heavy boots behind us brought an eagerness to my chest.

"Faster!" Norah cried.

Using the energy the vampire's blood had given me, I hurried my steps.

As Norah said, demons came at us—muttmaugs, dark-elths ... even Helia and Coyne appeared by our side. But we used our momentum to keep going. We pushed them out of our way with our vampire-like strength without losing speed.

"We're almost there," I shouted as the passage under the mountain grew bigger and closer to us.

As we reached the portal, I realized the demons had stopped attacking. Wary, I paused and looked back. From one of the balconies of the black palace, Brikan watched as Norah and I escaped. The demons, who before were attacking us, were now standing in the path, watching us.

Brikan was letting us go.

I didn't wonder why. I just pushed to my feet and started running again.

11

During a lunch break, the girls invaded my bedroom to cheer me up. Claire, Harper, and Ava brought me lunch and other supplies.

"Every night, you go to bed complaining that all of your muscles hurt," Claire said, resting a small massager device, pain relief pads, and a relaxing tea packet over my bed beside where I was seated.

"Try training for ten hours a day nonstop," I said, rolling my shoulders.

It was true, everything hurt. I spent most of the day practicing with Kristin, then the two of us joined Jasmin to practice the Infernal Curse. Despite Kristin's progress, she was still not in absolute control of her power. More than that, the three of us kept arguing, usually after some nasty comment from Jasmin, and training always ended in arguments.

"Here." Claire hopped on the bed behind me and started moving the massager around my shoulders and neck.

I moaned. "Holy shit, one could get used to this."

"You should apply these too." Harper offered me the pain relief pads. With a small smile, I took one from her and placed on my lower back. Heat seeped into me as the medicine started acting.

"I say you should drink some booze and go to bed early tonight," Ava suggested. She leaned back on my desk and crossed her arms. "That should help."

The thing was, as much as I wanted to go to bed early, I was also dreading it. For the last couple of days, Rey hadn't met me in my dreams and I was worried about him. I knew I was getting ahead of myself, since it could be that the Soul Bond simply didn't connect us each time we dozed off, but I couldn't stop thinking that it meant something more. What if Brikan was torturing him? What if he was dead?

My stomach tightened with the thought.

"Why aren't you eating?" Claire asked as she moved the massager down the length of my back. "You need to eat well if you're going to keep up this intense training up."

I had no appetite, but I knew she was right. Groaning, I picked up the big sandwich they had brought me and took a bite out of it.

"I still vote for booze tonight," Ava said. "We sure need it."

Harper shook her head. "And where do you suggest we find booze?"

"The entire campus is empty," Ava continued. "I bet if we go into one of the professor's townhouses in Dahlia Villa, we can find something."

The girls exchanged a glance, considering.

"Hm, no." I swallowed another bite of my sandwich. "You guys go ahead, but I think I'll feel worse if I drink. I do have to get up early tomorrow morning and do it all over again, you know."

Ava rolled her eyes. "Meanwhile, we just sit here and wait."

My brows curled down. "What is that supposed to mean?"

"Nothing," Ava snapped. She let out a long sigh. "Sorry … It's just that it has been a few days since everyone left and I'm bored out of my mind. You and your sisters practice all day, but the rest of us? We have nothing to do."

"That's not true," Harper said. "We've been watching movies and talking …" She paused. "Yeah, you're right. I'm getting bored too."

"Perhaps we should train too," Claire suggested.

We all looked at her as if she was an alien.

"Did I hear you right?" I asked, suddenly worried. Claire always hated training and any other physical activity.

Abandoning the massager, she scooted to the edge of the bed and sat beside me on the mattress. "I mean, we're all bored, and we know we'll need to fight King Brikan. It's not like I want to practice, but if we can at least keep ourselves from getting rusty."

Ava pursed her lips. "That is not a bad idea, actually. Although, I don't recommend her crazy training schedule." She pointed at me, the crazy one. "But sure. Why not practice for a couple hours each day?"

"I have another idea," Harper started, her voice low. "I was talking to my grandmother last night, and she said I probably have magic inside me. Since Claire has a lot of spell books, why don't you two help me with my magic while the others are busy?"

I felt slightly jealous. Damn it, I wanted to join them and help Harper with her magic too. But I was already doing something they couldn't. Now, it was my turn to let them go and not be mad at it.

"I think that's a great idea," I said, shoving my jealousy to the depths of my soul.

"I like it," Claire said with a smile. "I'll start gathering my books this afternoon!"

Ava shrugged. "Yeah. Whatever."

I took the last bite of my sandwich a second before my phone's alarm started ringing. With a sigh, I turned it off. "Time for me to go back." I stood from my bed and looked at each of the girls. "Thank you for lunch, the massage, and the pads."

"Our pleasure," Claire said. "Go kick ass."

I chuckled, though it was lacking any emotion. "I wish."

As I left my bedroom, I made a mental note to check on them before I blacked out in exhaustion tonight. I wanted to know how the magic training session went.

Outside, I took a deep breath of the crisp, early afternoon air, willing it to give me strength and keep me going. I looked around, glad most of the snow was finally clearing. It was the beginning of March, but the temperature was still too low in my opinion. As long as it didn't snow again, though, I would be satisfied.

When I arrived at the Hyacinth building, Jasmin and Kristin were already there, though each stood on opposite sides of the training room. In the last couple of days, Karen and Katrina started to extend their leash on Kristin. First, they came and stood outside in the hallway for as long as it took us to train. Then, they started coming, dropping her off, and leaving, though they came back every thirty minutes to check on Kristin. Now, they dropped her off and came back when Kristin texted them to let them know we were done. Which was better, since then there were fewer chances of Karen freaking out on us for any reason.

"You know," I said, walking to the center of the room. "I believe our magic will only work together once we all accept each other and treat each other better. Like friends."

Jasmin snorted. "Right, because I'm here to be nice and make friends."

Seriously, Jasmin knew how to get on my nerves. In a way, she reminded me of Ava, when she used to be more annoying. Though with Jasmin, I didn't know if she would ever change and let us get close to her.

I opened my mouth to say something about teamwork and all that crap—I was about to wing it—when my phone chimed. I picked up and read the message.

"It's Fiona," I told the others. "She'll be a little late."

"And what the hell are we supposed to do now?" Jasmin asked, practically barking.

"We could try practicing by ourselves," I said.

"I'm up for it," Kristin said.

"Well, I'm not." Jasmin examined her nails. "I could use a longer break." She started walking to the door, but after taking two steps, she stopped. "What are you doing here?"

I whirled to the door and saw Tanner entering the room.

"I just wanted to check on you all," he said, with a soft grin.

When they first met, Jasmin and Kristin had no idea who Tanner was and vice versa, so back then I had to explain everything. So far, Tanner had spent more time with Harvey and the girls, but once in a while, he popped in, and for some reason, Jasmin became even more nasty whenever he was around.

"So, has Fiona spilled the beans about the prophecy?" Tanner asked. "You guys spend so much time together. She has to say something."

"She didn't," I confessed. "She said that for the whole thing to play out favorably, the three of us will have to figure out what it means by ourselves."

Tanner's nose wrinkled. "I gather that's not going well."

Jasmin scoffed. "What do you think?"

I waved my hand at Jasmin. "Ignore her. All she does is scoff, snort, and complain."

"Hey!" Jasmin puffed her chest and faced me. "I'm here, am I not? I'm helping!"

"Whatever you say," I muttered, annoyed by her behavior.

Jasmin stepped in front of me. "Who are you to talk to me like that? You looked like a damned princess being pampered by all your friends, and with your overprotective mother and—"

"I wonder," Kristin said, her voice low, but with a shrill tone. "What will happen once we defeat Brikan?"

I frowned. "What do you mean?"

"I mean, so the underworld will be ours?" she asked. "I don't want any part of the underworld."

"Me neither," I said.

"I want a big part of it, but I sure as hell don't want to be queen of the underworld," Jasmin said.

The three of us looked at Tanner.

His eyes widened. "What? What's with those faces?"

"Remember when we talked about this several months ago?" Rey, Claire, and I had helped Tanner escape the academy. We talked briefly about the underworld's ownership. At that time, Tanner said he didn't want to rule either. "Have you changed your mind?"

"Hm." He pursed his lips. "Not really. But ... I might be convinced, if that's your idea."

"How about if you become the new king of the underworld, Tanner?" I continued with my thought process. "You give a part of the underworld to Jasmin, though you can supervise it to make sure she isn't doing anything wrong." She glared at me, and I glared at her. "And you have to give the three of us the ability to come knock you off the throne if you start running things into the ground."

Kristin nodded. "I like that."

Jasmin looked at her long nails again. "Yeah. I guess it works."

Tanner opened his mouth, then closed it again. "Hm. Are you sure? I mean, I'm honored, but the three of you are the Demon Kissed Queens and—"

"None of us want to rule," I said, cutting him off. "If you're not willing, we'll figure something out."

He frowned. "I want to. I mean, I want to try." He rolled back his shoulders and stood straighter. "I'll try."

"Now that that is all done and solved, can we do something?" Jasmin asked. "Even practice by ourselves. I'm so bored, I'll do that."

That was unexpected, but I wouldn't complain, lest she give up. But first, I said to Tanner, "You're staying, right?"

He nodded. "Yup."

"Good. Then hang around. Do whatever. We can all have dinner together tonight and talk more." I waved at him and turned back to Kristin and Jasmin, ready to start training.

IN THE END, FIONA DIDN'T COME ALL AFTERNOON. JASMIN endured training with us for almost an hour, even though she complained and bickered most of the time, then I let Kristin take a ten-minute break before we practiced by ourselves. I had to keep in mind she was only twelve and I couldn't push her too hard, even if she wanted to. Besides being a kid, she wasn't used to the intense workload.

I had told myself we would practice for only thirty minutes more when my phone rang. Claire's name flashed on the screen. I ignored it, because she knew we were busy, but she called again.

I frowned, thinking that if she insisted, it was because she had something important to tell me.

"Hey, what's up?" I asked as I answered the phone.

"Hey, hm, you should come outside," she said.

"We're training. What is this about?"

"Erin, just come outside. It's kinda urgent."

And she hung up on me.

I stared at the phone. "What the hell?"

Kristin approached me. "What happened?"

"I don't know," I told her. "I'm supposed to go outside. Want to come with me?"

She shrugged. "Sure."

Together, we walked out of the classroom and exited the building. Before me, the courtyard extended, the Blackthorn tree as majestic as ever. Above, clouds rolled in, blocking the last of the sun rays for the afternoon.

Claire, Harper, and Ava stood on the right side of the courtyard, at the steps of the Statice building. Whatever it was, it didn't seem urgent as they were just standing there, doing nothing. Frowning, I descended the stone stairs and followed the path leading to them.

And that was when I saw.

A tall figure across the courtyard, walking from the Aster building directly toward me.

My heart stopped and my steps faltered.

It was Rey.

Rey was here.

12

REY

I HAD BEEN WAITING FOR THIS MOMENT SINCE I ARRIVED IN THE underworld. The moment I saw Erin across the courtyard, my heart expanded and I could barely breathe. When she saw me, she almost tripped on her feet.

I ran toward her. Two seconds later, Erin ran to me too.

We crashed onto each other, our arms and legs entwined and our chests glued on one another.

"Holy shit, you're here," she whispered in my ear. "You're really here."

"I'm here, and I'm never leaving your side again." I pressed a kiss to her cheek. On her nose. On her lips.

Time slowed down. I pressed my mouth to hers and kissed her. She inhaled sharply, her nails sinking into my arms, as she parted her lips for me and let me in. I jumped. I free fell into her, knowing she was my home, my life, my heart, my soul. Erin was mine and I was hers, and even when the devil separated us, our love would go on.

I moved my mouth against hers, so desperately I was sure

her lips would be bruised later on. Finally, after a long while, we were both breathless. We pulled back, but didn't let go of each other.

Erin's eyes skimmed over my face, her hands hovering over me. "How?" She shook her head. "What happened? How are you here?"

"Your mother sent Norah to help me escape," I told her.

Her eyes bulged. "My mother? She didn't tell me anything."

"Probably because she didn't want you to be more worried than you already were." I pressed my hand over her breast, right where I knew the Soul Bond mark rested. "I'm sorry for making you worry."

Tears brimmed Erin's golden eyes. "You're here now. That's all that matters." She embraced me again, and I sank into her, just glad to be with her.

But there was one thing bothering me. "Erin, when Norah and I were escaping, Brikan saw it and he let us go."

When she pulled back, she was frowning. "That's not like him."

"I know, and I'm worried about that."

Erin shrugged. "You know what? I can't worry about it. I won't let anything spoil my suddenly wonderful mood, not even that." She smiled at me. Then she looked around. "Where did everyone go?"

I followed her line of sight. Sure enough, her friends were nowhere to be seen. "I guess they didn't want to witness us jump each other."

Erin chuckled. "Well, speaking of jumping ..." She tightened her hands around mine. Suddenly, the world spun around us. When it settled a second later, we were in the empty living room of my townhouse. "We could use a little more private time, don't you think?" Then, she let go of my hands. "Unless ... I mean. You must be tired and hurt. Probably starving." She turned to the kitchen. "Why don't you go take a shower while I prepare dinner, then—"

"Erin." I grabbed her wrist and tugged her to me. A gasp fled from her lips as she crashed into me, her hands on my chest. "Just shut up." Sliding my hands around her back, I leaned into her and claimed her mouth again.

Erin let out a sigh as she kissed me back, matching my desperate rhythm perfectly. With deft hands, I stripped her of her training uniform, while backing her to the wall.

Then I showed her just how much I missed her.

WE SPENT MOST OF THE NIGHT IN BED—MAKING LOVE, JUST holding each other, eating dinner, talking. If I had my way, I would never leave here, and I would never take my hands from her. Even if it was my pinky touching her pinky. I needed to feel her warmth, to hear her breathe, to smell her sweet scent.

With her head resting on my arm, Erin traced her fingertip over one of the many thin lines covering my shoulders.

"I'm so sorry for what he did to you," she whispered.

My brow furrowed. "It doesn't matter now," I said, though I couldn't lie to myself that I was a little worried about the scars on my back. What if Erin found me repulsive now? But so far, she had been amazing as always. And now she caressed my scars, as if they were an extension of me. "Now he can't hurt me anymore."

"Damn straight!" She dipped her chin, moving her cheek against my arm.

"How have things been here?" I asked, knowing I had missed a lot.

Erin let out a long breath. "Not great. Fiona, who by the way is Harper's grandmother, Francine, told us we need to use something called the Infernal Curse to defeat Brikan. And for that, we need to unite our magic and fight him as one, but Kristin had never used her powers before, so there's a learning curve."

"She's too young," I said, remembering the little girl standing with her two older sisters, eager to help, but being held back.

"I know. I think so too, but there isn't much I can do about that. I can't change the mark from her wrist to Karen's, for example. But Kristin is willing to do anything, but Jasmin is a pain in the ass. I also think she doesn't like Kristin getting involved. That, or she simply doesn't like Kristin. Regardless, she's always complaining and bickering about everything. It's annoying."

"What I can do to help?"

She cocked one eyebrow. "You know what? We haven't done it in a while, but you and I were able to unite our powers before."

"Because of the Soul Bond."

"Right. We should be able to do it again. That way, we can show them how to do it. Even if it's a little different, since you're my twin soul and they are my sisters, but still. Perhaps seeing it being done will help them get an idea of how it's supposed to be, what it's supposed to look like."

I nodded. "We can definitely do that."

She smiled at me, her face so radiant, so beautiful, it

made my heart clench. Slowly, she brought her hand around my shoulders, down my collarbone, until her fingertips traced the mark on my chest. "You know, once the Soul Bond is restored, it becomes stronger than ever. I think that's why we could meet in our dreams. I had hoped that I would be able to sense you and find you once it was restored, so I could rescue you. That was my plan at least. But you were faster and escaped by yourself."

"I didn't want to be a damsel in distress, and I didn't want to cause you any distress either." I glanced at the mark, twin to mine, on her skin. "How did you do it? How did you restore the Soul Bond?"

"When we first met Fiona, I told her I wanted to find a way to rescue you, so she suggested restoring the Soul Bond." She went on, telling me about the risks, the cleansing ritual, the ceremony, the angel.

My breath caught. "You were ready to lay down your life for me."

"Wouldn't you do the same for me?"

I didn't hesitate. "I would." My heart swelled, becoming bigger than my chest. Fuck, how I loved this woman. There were no words for it. She was everything to me, plain and simple. I tightened my arms around her, bringing her closer to me. "I love you," I whispered.

She lifted her chin, aligning her face with mine. "I love you more."

Slowly, I brushed my lips against hers. Now that the desperation of our reunion had passed, I would savor her, take in her scent, her taste, mark her in my soul, lock her in my heart.

I rolled over her, pressing my naked body to hers. "You're mine," I said with a growl.

"That I am," she whispered, running her nails on my back, sending a delicious shiver down my spine. "And you're mine."

I brushed my lips on hers and said against her mouth, "Forever."

13

WITH REY'S HELP, KRISTIN, JASMIN, AND I WERE ABLE TO UNITE our magic. It took a couple of days and a lot of swearing, but now, two weeks after Rey's return, we were finally doing it. Once the training started, my sisters and I immediately joined our powers and hit all the targets Fiona put in front of us.

In the past two weeks, things had changed around campus. Classes resumed, but the campus still felt empty since only a low percentage of the students came back. My mother had tried making the academy more secure, so parents wouldn't feel afraid to send their kids back. She even had Fiona create a magical shield around the academy—we knew it wouldn't stop Brikan, but it might slow him down and warn us, giving us time to evacuate everyone. Even so, the world was afraid of Brikan.

I couldn't blame them.

Although my friends had gone back to classes, I hadn't since I had to train with my sisters all day. My mother promised that once we defeated Brikan and things went back to normal, she would help me catch up so I wasn't behind.

On a Thursday morning, I stayed in Rey's bed while he got up and went to his first class of the day. He still had classes to teach, even with the low turnout. I should be up and ready for training too, but I had sent a text to Fiona, Kristin, and Jasmin, asking to postpone the practice until mid-morning. I had been pushing myself hard these past couple of weeks, and it showed. I dragged my feet to and from the Hyacinth building so often that I ended up napping in my plate during lunch breaks, and I hit the mattress way too early at night. I wanted to stay up and enjoy having Rey by my side, but had settled for simply snuggling with him and passing out.

Because Brikan could literally attack us at any time, we weren't even taking the weekends off.

But we needed to, otherwise we would break down. With that in mind, I pushed the warm blankets aside and forced myself to get dressed. I was planning on eating too, but once I got to the kitchen, my stomach turned, and I almost gagged at the sight and smell of food. Seriously, this could only be a side effect of pushing myself too hard.

Ignoring the feeling and the food, I trudged on. I left Rey's townhouse and went to the classroom where the girls and I usually trained. Kristin was already there, by herself. A moment later, Fiona arrived. But Jasmin was late, as usual.

To pass the time, Kristin practiced her magic under Fiona's and my surveillance. She conjured bolts of darkfire and threw them at the targets spread through the room, in quick succession. The targets had been painted with numbers—one through five. Which meant number one should be hit with a small, weak bolt, and number five should be hit with a strong bolt.

"She's getting better," Fiona said in a low voice.

"She is." I nodded. "Which is good, because we need to make more progress."

"I know." Fiona glanced at me. "I actually prepared something different for today."

I cocked my eyebrow at her, but she didn't tell me. Finally, Jasmin arrived. Tired of everything, I didn't complain; otherwise she would snap at me and we would end up arguing again.

Kristin and I met her at the center of the room, while Fiona went to the storage room in the back. She paused at the closed door and looked at us. "Today, we'll start a different exercise." The door rattled and a low growl followed. Kristin took a step back.

"What ...?" I sucked in a sharp breath. "You have a demon in there."

Fiona nodded. "A lesser demon. I want you to defeat it. Together."

Kristin's face blanched, and Jasmin rolled her eyes. "Look here, old lady. If you think I'm going to—"

A ripple of powers coursed through the room and Jasmin shut her mouth.

"I'm old and powerful, and because of that, I demand respect," Fiona said, with a bite to her usual voice. "Now, hitting static targets will only get you so far. The best way to progress is fighting an actual demon. We'll start with lesser demons. One first, two next, then three. Once you can defeat five lesser demons in less than ten seconds, we'll progress to neutral demons. One, then two, then three, and so on. Hopefully, you three will work together and this will go smoothly. The best-case scenario would be for you to defeat five higher demons within the next month. Then, and only then, you'll be ready for the Infernal Curse."

I shook my head. What she was saying made sense, and I understood the urgency of the situation. We didn't have time to go inch by inch. We had to go mile by mile. But ... what the hell? Kristin had never fought a real demon, not by herself, and despite the methodic training so far, Jasmin didn't really look like a team player. The moment a demon rushed us, she would dart the opposite way, and let us be bait.

I opened my mouth to tell Fiona my thoughts, but she opened the door.

A single garrimp ran out of the storage room. The waist high, gray-skinned monster paused for a moment, looking at us with its yellow catlike eyes. It bared its pointy teeth at us before stomping its large feet on the mat, running toward us.

Kristin froze. Jasmin took several steps back, just as I thought.

"Come on, girls!" I yelled. I summoned my power. As it filled my veins and coiled in my core, a wave of dizziness assaulted me. Pushing against it, I threw my hands out and sent a bolt of darkfire at the little imp.

But the bolt never came.

Instead, I fell on my knees, my stomach contracting in pain, and gagging as if I had drunk too much last night and was now paying for it.

"Erin!" I heard someone call as the garrimp jumped over me, sharp teeth snapping. I fell back, out of breath and dizzy, with the garrimp pressing over my chest.

I swatted it to the side, and rolled on to my stomach. But

before I could drag myself away, pain rushed through me, making me curl into myself. My breath grew shallow, and I felt way too hot.

"Erin, talk to me," someone said.

I blinked, trying to force myself to focus.

"Breathe, just breathe."

Shutting my eyes, I inhaled deeply, then let the air out slowly. I repeated that a couple of times, and the dizziness and pain went away. Once I was sure I wouldn't throw up, I opened my eyes again. Fiona and Rey knelt beside me on the mat, their eyes huge with worry. Behind them, Kristin and Jasmin spied at me.

"W-what happened?" I asked, pushing up. Rey caught my arm and helped me to my feet. The world swayed and Rey tightened his hold on me.

"I was going to ask you that," Rey said. "You were writhing on the floor when I arrived. What happened?"

"I don't know," I confessed. "I was about to attack the garrimp when—" My eyes bulged. "The garrimp!"

"It's dead," Fiona said. "When you fell and it came for you, I used my magic to put it back in storage."

"I'm sorry." My shoulders deflated. "We couldn't do the exercise because of me."

"That's what you're worried about?" Rey asked, his tone laced with worry. "What happened?" he asked again.

I shrugged. "I really don't know. I felt ... dizzy, and a sudden pain hit me hard."

Fiona frowned. "Where does it hurt?"

"The pain and the dizziness are gone now, but it started here." I touched my center, right above my solar plexus. "In my gut, I would say."

"Maybe we should go to the infirmary," Rey suggested, tugging me forward.

"No, I'm fine now." I pulled my arm from his hold, to show him I could stand on my own. "I have no idea what that was, but it's gone now. We can keep practicing."

Rey regarded me with uncertain eyes, but he didn't protest.

"Are you sure?" Fiona asked.

I nodded. We had no time to waste. "Yeah, let's do this."

Rey and Fiona retreated to the side of the room, while Kristin, Jasmin, and I stood in the center. I took a deep breath and rolled my shoulders.

Fiona extended her hand toward the storage door. "Ready?"

"Wait," I said. I turned to the girls. "Kristin, I know this is scary, but don't worry. We won't let anything happen to you. As for you, Jasmin, I saw you retreating, leaving Kristin and I to deal with the demon by ourselves."

She gasped, outraged. "I didn't—"

"Save it," I cut her off. "I saw it. The spell won't work if you don't stand your ground and help us."

"You're acting like you are the powerful witch calling the shots," Jasmin muttered.

"I heard that!" Fiona said.

Jasmin rolled her eyes.

I shook my head, then tried to focus. Demon, power, spell. We could do this. "Ready," I told Fiona.

She twisted her hand, and from afar, the door opened.

The garrimp didn't waste time. It came at us with incredible sped. This time, Jasmin didn't move and Kristin lifted her arms, ready to summon her magic. Good.

I called my magic. I didn't have time to feel it as the pain and dizziness came back, stronger this time.

My knees buckled and I fell on the mat.

The world became dark.

14

I JUMPED INTO ACTION. WITHOUT BATTING A LASH, I obliterated the garrimp with a powerful bolt of darkfire, while racing to Erin.

I skidded to her side and gently touched her face. "Erin? Wake up. Erin!"

"The infirmary," Fiona said.

I scooped Erin in my arms and raced to the Iris building, where the infirmary was located. While running, I glanced down at Erin, a dead weight against me. My chest constricted with worry. What the fuck was going on?

"Please, hang on," I pleaded.

At the infirmary, I didn't wait to be called on or for someone to come to me. I barged into the back area and deposited Erin in one of the many hospital beds. Cecile, the physician, was gone. She had left a while ago and hadn't come back. But Peggy, a demon hunter who served as one of the physicians for the Blackthorn Hunters, had taken her place, even if temporarily.

"What the hell is going on?" she asked, coming to meet me.

"It's Erin, Martha's daughter," I told her, not sure if the hunter knew about Erin, or not. "She was practicing with her sisters when she fell. It happened twice. The first time, she said she felt pain here." I pointed to the top of my stomach. "And dizzy. She said she was dizzy."

Peggy pushed me aside and leaned over Erin's bed. She examined Erin, checking her heartbeat, her pressure, her temperature, and more.

"Her heartbeat is a little fast, but it seems to be slowing down." Peggy lifted Erin's shirt and pressed her stomach. "I don't feel anything wrong in here either. I can do more exams, but right now, I don't know what is wrong with her."

"I think I know," Fiona said as she entered the infirmary. Kristin and Jasmin were right behind her.

"What do you mean?" I asked.

Fiona stood on the other side of the bed and placed a heavy hand on Erin's forehead. She closed her eyes and inhaled deeply. I felt her magic whirling around Erin, like a little hook searching for fishes.

With a sharp breath, Fiona's eyes snapped open. "As I thought." She shifted her gaze to me. "Erin was cursed."

AFTER FIONA'S DIAGNOSIS, I WAITED UNTIL PEGGY GAVE ERIN an IV with fluids, since she was weak and probably dehydrated, then moved her to my townhouse. I watched her like a hawk, though I felt impatient. Who cursed her? Why? How? What was this fucking curse? I had clue.

Erin soon woke up, but she was too weak to stand on her own, so I declared she was on bedrest until further notice.

"But I have a war to fight!" she protested.

I loved her, but I ignored her protests. How could she fight a fucking war if she couldn't stand upright and summon her magic?

That evening, Martha came to my townhouse to check on Erin. "I'm sorry it took me so long to come. I had a million things to deal with." She sat on my bed beside a sleeping Erin. "How is she?"

"Weak," I said, standing at the foot of the bed, my arms crossed. "She wakes up, complains about being in bed, drinks a little water, takes a small bite of something, and promptly goes back to sleep."

Martha touched Erin's forehead, as if checking for her temperature. "Fiona told me it's a curse."

"That's what she said, though she can't figure out what curse, and when it was cast upon her."

Martha let out a long breath. "We should try finding a master curse-breaker." I frowned. I hadn't heard that term in so long. I had only met one master curse-breaker in my long life and it had been decades ago. The man had been a famous demon hunter who died a tragic death at the hands of duclaws, curse bearing demons. "The real Ivan was one," she muttered.

I snorted. King Brikan had killed Ivan years ago, and impersonated him to come to the academy at the beginning of the semester, all to get close to Erin.

"You don't know of any other?" I asked.

She shook her head. "No. Being a master curse-breaker isn't a common thing. But I'll find one." She pulled out her phone from the pocket of her suit. "I'll contact everyone I know until I find one."

I appreciated her initiative, and I really hoped she found someone, but I couldn't just sit here and wait for a master curse-breaker to show up.

My brows curled down. "Do you mind staying with her for a couple of hours?"

"Of course I don't." Martha narrowed her eyes. "What are you going?"

"To help the others."

***

As I expected, I found Claire, Harper, Ava, Harvey, and Tanner in the academy's library—the locked section. They sat around three long tables right in the center, with dozens of books spread around them.

"I knew I would find you here," I said as I joined them. I grabbed one of the books from the pile and skimmed through it.

"How is she?" Claire asked.

"Weak," I repeated the same answer I had given to Martha. I frowned, looking at the book in my hands. It was titled *The Hidden World of the Supernaturals*. "Have you guys found anything?"

"It's hard to find something when we don't exactly know what we are looking for," Harvey said. "All we know is it's a curse that makes her violently ill."

"From what I could see, it manifested each time she uses her magic," I told them.

"So, it made her dizzy and caused her pain when she used

her magic?" Ava asked. She was seated on the other side of the desk, her feet crossed and resting on the table.

"That's about it," I said. Which wasn't much.

For the next hour, I skimmed through a dozen books, trying to find the damn curse that had been inflicted on Erin, but no luck. There were millions of curses listed in these books, but none of them matched what was happening to Erin.

"I found something!" Claire shouted.

We all rushed to her and spied her book from her over her shoulder. "This chapter explains how to perfect a general curse-breaking ritual. I have no idea if it'll work, but maybe we could try it."

"Does it have any side effects?" I asked.

Claire shook her head. "It doesn't seem to. And from what I read, it really is very straight-forward. I don't think it can create a negative effect either way."

I held my breath, quickly weighing the pros and cons. Pros: if it worked, we got rid of Erin's curse. Cons: if it didn't work, Erin went on with the fucking curse, but at least, it seemed the curse couldn't get worse.

"Let's try it," I said.

Claire snapped her head to me. "Right now?"

"If everything we need is available, yes, right now."

Claire rattled off a short list of ingredients and told Harper, Ava, and Harvey to go find them. We put the books down, and walked out of the library, while agreeing to meet back at my townhouse in about thirty minutes.

But we all stopped just outside the Iris building.

"I was looking for you, Rey Lowe." Daerman, leader of the half-demon camp and Vaira's boyfriend, stood in our path.

His eyes were bloodshot and his hair was disheveled, as if he hadn't slept much lately.

I frowned. "Daerman. How did you get in here?"

"I just told the guards I was here to visit my friend, Professor Rey," he said, his voice dripping with sarcasm. "They told me visiting hours were over, but I insisted."

"What do you want?" I asked, aware that Claire, Harper, Ava, Harvey, and Tanner were right behind me, staring at Daerman. As far as I knew, they had never met the half-demon.

"What I want ..." Daerman shifted his weight. "I want my woman back. My people." He bared his teeth at me. "You killed them all!"

I took one step closer, sorry for the guy. "I apologize for recruiting them into the Dark Knight Unit, but unfortunately, I couldn't have known what Randall, then Crimson, had in mind. I didn't know they would try to kill all half-demons."

"They didn't *try* to kill the half-demons. They killed them all, and it's your fault!" He pointed at me. "You and that bitch of yours, Erin. You two destroyed my people, my home, my love ... everything I had!"

I raised my hands, taking another step closer. "Daerman, I'm sor—"

A darkfire bolt zipped at me. I was able to shift to the side and avoid it by one inch. The bolt exploded on the wall behind me, leaving a black mark on the gray stones. My friends gasped, and I clenched my fists.

Daerman threw another bolt, but I raised a shield in front of my friends and me.

"Coward!" the half-demon cried, sending more bolts, faster, stronger. The shield shimmered, losing its force.

My friends summoned their Dawnblades. I dropped the shield and did the same.

Daerman's gaze surveyed us. "Mark my words," he snarled. "This is not the end. You and Erin ... you'll pay for what you've done." He threw a last darkfire ball at us.

I easily cut it with my sword, making it fade in the air.

By then, Daerman ran.

Harvey and Tanner were the first to sprint after him.

"Leave him be," I said.

Harvey halted right away, but Tanner took a few steps more before actually stopping. "What the hell, man? He's getting away."

I exhaled. "He's just hurt. We need to let him be. Eventually, he'll move on."

At least, that was what I hoped.

Besides, I didn't have time to worry about a deranged half-demon right now. Not with Erin suffering from an unknown curse, and with the war against Brikan looming over our heads. If, after we solved our current problems, Daerman was still making loose threats, I'd deal with the situation.

But for now, I focused on Erin.

"Are we still doing the ritual tonight?" Ava asked, tapping her boots on the stone pavement.

I nodded. "Yes, we are."

15

ERIN

"ONE MORE SPOONFUL."

"Mom!" I groaned. Since I woke a few minutes ago, she had been trying to shove water and food in my mouth. I drank a few sips of water and ate two spoonfuls of the noodle chicken soup Rey had left for me, but I didn't feel good enough to eat any more. "I'm fine. Just stop."

She dropped the spoon in the bowl on the nightstand and glared at me. "You're not fine. If you were fine, you wouldn't be passing out."

"But that's not because I'm not eating. That's because of a freaking curse," I snapped.

When I first woke up after passing out in the Hyacinth building, Rey told me Fiona had sensed a curse on me. Which baffled me. Who cursed me, and when? I raked my mind, trying to think when I could have been alone with anyone who didn't like me and how they could have cast a curse on me without me knowing, but I couldn't think of one single moment. The only time I had been alone with an enemy had been when I faced Brikan in the arena, though I hadn't been truly alone with him. Rey had been there with me, though he had been spelled by Brikan. Also, there had been dozens of people around the arena, outside the barrier that Brikan had created. If he had cursed me then, others would have seen it, and I would have known, right?

The sounds of footsteps reached my ears. My mother stood from the bed and stood beside it, as if she were my bodyguard. What did she think, that evil would arrive making a lot of noise?

Rey entered his bedroom, followed by Claire, who was carrying a heavy, leather-bound book.

"What's going on?" I asked them.

Rey sat on the mattress beside me. "How are you feeling?"

I shrugged. "I'm okay," I lied. I wasn't okay. I felt weak and nauseated. My body was sore as if I had exercised too much, or taken a beating. And every once in a while, a wave of pain whipped through my body. "But tell me, what's going on?"

"I found a curse-breaking spell," Claire declared, holding out the book.

"Let me see," my mother said. She stood beside Claire as my friend flipped through the pages and showed her the spell. "Hm. It's generic, but since we don't know who did this and how, I don't see why we can't try." She looked to me. "Are you okay with that?"

"Hell, yes," I said, my voice thin. "Anything that makes me feel better."

Rey rested his hand on my leg. I could feel his warmth, even with the blanket in between. "Are you sure? If you're not feeling well, we can do this tomorrow."

I shook my head and threw the blankets aside. "No, let's do it now. The sooner we try this, the sooner I'll get rid of it."

Holding my arm like a vice grip, Rey helped me to my

feet. Slowly, we made our way down the stairs. I felt like an old lady with motor impairments, and I hated how the three of them—Rey, Claire, and my mother—were hovering over me as if I would collapse at any second.

Since we didn't know the extent of this curse, I didn't complain. I just went with the flow, hiding how annoyed and frustrated I was with this situation.

As we exited Rey's townhouse into the dark and cold night, Harper, Ava, Harvey, and Tanner rounded the corner into the Dahlia Villa and walked to us. Harper had a bunch of herbs in her hands, Ava and Harvey had a couple of glass vials each, and Tanner carried a dead rat by the tail.

I wrinkled my nose, remembering when my mother made me practice dark magic. She would kill rats so I could steal their life force. So disgusting.

"What do we do with these?" Harper asked, as they halted in front of us.

"Here," Claire walked out a few steps, into the wider side of the stone pavement. "Bring them here and I'll arrange them."

Leaning against Rey, I watched as Claire mixed the herbs, the contents of the vials, and the rat's blood into a small bowl. Then, she used the mixture to paint a small circle on the ground, like a witch's summoning circle. She drew the symbols around the perimeter, just like it was depicted in the book, then beckoned me forward.

Rey held me up, but I shook my head at him. "I'd like to do this alone." Or rather, at least to try to do this alone. Being dependent on others was killing me.

Knowing I needed to hold on to some of my pride, Rey pressed his lips together, as if keeping in his worry, and he let me go. I dragged my feet to the center of the circle, each step painful and tiring. Holy shit, I was probably ninety-nine and didn't even know it.

Claire looked at me, a deep knot in her forehead. "All you have to do is stand here. Is that okay?"

With each passing second, my legs grew heavier. But I nodded. "Just do whatever the hell you have to do."

She stepped out of the circle and passed the book to Harper. She had taken Claire's advice and started practicing magic between classes. Sometimes, after training with me and my sisters, Fiona would stop by and check on her progress. As far as I knew, Harper had been able to access her magic and control it, but she was afraid of using too much at a time, so she over-controlled it. Which was better than overusing it, I guess.

Harper held on to the book, her fingers curling around the thick, leather cover, and inhaled deeply. "All right," she said. Then, she launched on a sort of chant in a weird language.

The circle reacted instantly, the lines shining bright against the gray stones underneath. The magic pulsated around me, until it reached me, licking up my legs and enveloping my body. The magic pressed against me until it was inside me, moving, flowing, searching.

Dizziness assaulted me again and I stepped to the side, almost losing my balance.

Rey stepped forward, to catch me in case I fell, but Claire stopped him. "Don't! If you go inside the circle, the ritual will be broken."

I was too dazed to see his reaction, but I bet he cursed under his breath while curling his hands, trying to contain himself.

The magic wrapped around my insides and tugged. I

inhaled sharply, shocked by its force. If it didn't find the curse, what would it do? Rip my organs apart? Because that was what that tug felt like.

The spell swirling around my core, my gut, and a low humming started inside me, like a vibration of sorts. A battle. The curse against the spell.

There was no contest. The curse slugged the magic like a person blowing out a candle. The magic faded away, and the shine from the circle died.

The dizziness came back and my legs folded underneath me.

"Erin!" This time Rey ran into the circle and hooked his arm around my waist before my knees touched the ground. "What is it? What do you feel? Did it work?"

I shook my head. "The curse was too strong," I whispered, too weak to even speak.

"Fuck," he muttered. He ran a hand over my head, before pulling me up in his arms. "It's okay. Just rest now."

I didn't want to sleep so soon, so easily, but whatever that ritual had been, it had drained me of the little energy I had. Against my will, I closed my eyes and fell asleep.

WHEN I WOKE, IT WAS EARLY MORNING, AND REY WAS GETTING ready to go out. He put on the jacket of his suit and turned to me. "Good morning." He sat on the mattress and touched my forehead. "How are you feeling?"

"The same," I said, not wanting to elaborate. The same meant shitty. With much effort, I sat up. I propped a pillow behind me and leaned back. "Going to class?"

"Now that I see you're awake and well, I think so," he said.

"Unless you're not feeling well and want me to stay." He checked his phone. "I know your mother has an important meeting to go to, and the others have class ... but I can stay with you until someone can take my place."

I tsked. "Nah, I'm okay."

Rey's gray eyes turned almost silver with worry. It had been the look stamped on his pretty face for the past couple of days, and even though he was still handsome, I hated being the one to give him such trouble. "I don't like leaving you alone."

"As you said, it'll be only for a little while. I think I can survive." I reached for my phone on the nightstand. "I promise to text you if something happens." I forced a small smile on my lips. "Go. Teach your class. Do something for the both of us."

Rey reached for my hand. He laced his fingers on mine. "Don't just text me if something happens. Text me every five minutes, letting me know you're fine."

I chuckled. "Five minutes? No. Half an hour."

"Ten minutes," he rebuked.

"Twenty."

"Fine, fifteen. Every fifteen minutes. I won't accept less than that."

I rolled my eyes. "Yes, sir. Fifteen minutes."

He pointed to the nightstand on his side of the bed, where a tray with breakfast waited for me. "Eat something."

"I will, sir," I teased, pushing his hand away. "Now go before you're late."

With a groan, Rey planted a quick peck on my lips before standing up. He checked his suit in the mirror one more time, then marched out of the bedroom.

I glanced at the tray and wrinkled my nose. Nope, no

stomach for food. I rolled on to my side and lay back on the bed. I was sick and tired of staying in bed like an invalid, but what else could I do? How could I fight against a curse when I couldn't even use my magic?

This sucked hard.

A moment later, I heard the front door closing. Rey had left for his class, and I instantly missed him. I knew he couldn't, and shouldn't, babysit me all day, but I hated that he was leaving me here alone.

Since I had nothing else to do, I closed my eyes, trying to sleep again. Perhaps if I rested as my body seemed to want it, I would feel stronger soon.

As if.

I must had fallen asleep and woken up hours later, because I heard the front door opening, and then footsteps coming up the stairs. Rey was back. From what I remembered of his schedule, he didn't have any classes this afternoon and he could stay with me. Perhaps we could snuggle and watch a movie together, while pretending there was no curse, there was no magic, there no underworld, or Supreme Demon, and Demon Kissed Queens ... just Rey and me.

I sat up and smiled as he stepped into the bedroom.

Only it wasn't Rey.

16

I was almost at the Statice building when I realized I left one of my notebooks back at my house. My mind had been so scattered lately, I would forget my head because if it wasn't attached to my neck. It was the curse on Erin, making her too weak to train with her sisters, and if they didn't train together, they wouldn't be able to perform the Infernal Curse and defeat Brikan. A giant snowball that only got bigger and worse.

Also, the fact that Brikan watched as Norah and I escaped from the underworld still bothered me. Why the fuck did he do that?

I paused outside the building, pondering if I should wing it and teach class without my notebook, but with my mind so busy, I doubted I would do a good job if I didn't follow my notes.

So, I rushed back to my townhouse to grab the notebook before my class started.

When I approached my house, I paused. Something felt

wrong. I reached the knob, but I didn't have to twist it, or even unlock the door, because it swung open.

A crash came from upstairs followed by a growl and a scream.

Heart in my throat, I dropped my things and raced up the stairs, climbing four at a time. At the landing, I didn't pause. I summoned my Dawnblade and burst into my room.

Daerman stood in the middle of the room, holding Erin up against the wall with his darkfire wrapped around her neck.

Red rage filled my veins and covered my eyes.

I didn't think; I acted. Without a word, I swung my sword wide and cut across Daerman's back. His magic faltered and Erin fell to the floor, gasping loudly. Teeth bared, the half-demon turned to me. "Now I'm going to kill you both."

"Not if I kill you first."

He summoned two bolts of darkfire. For half a second, I considered playing fair—to let go of my sword and use dark-fire too. But he had sneaked into my house and used his power on Erin, who could barely stand on her own. What if I hadn't come back? What if I had decided to present my class without my notebook?

I couldn't think about that.

More enraged by the second, I waved my free hand, sending a wave of darkfire at Daerman as he was about to throw his power at me. The wave hit him in the chest, making him drop his magic and stagger back. Without missing a beat, I stepped forward and plunged my Dawnblade in his chest.

Daerman's eyes went wide. "No," he muttered. "I have to make you suffer."

"You did." When he hurt Erin, he had hurt me.

I pulled out my sword and stepped back. His knees hit the floor, and a moment later, his body fell at the feet.

And I rushed to Erin, who was panting on the other side of the room, trying to stand up, but too weak to do so.

"Hey, I'm here." I scooped her up in my arms and turned to the bed. Then, I paused. No, I wouldn't put her down in the bed with a body beside it. So I took her downstairs to the kitchen and placed her on one of the stools, while I cursed myself for not having more furniture in this fucking house. Why hadn't I bought a couch or a bed for the guest bedroom? I brushed her hair away and examined her neck. It was red and angry. I hissed, knowing it would darken before it got better. "How are you feeling? What's hurting?"

"I'm okay," she whispered, her voice rough. "Still weak, but I'm okay now."

I punched the counter. "I should have been here. I shouldn't have left you alone."

She grabbed my arms and pulled me closer. "We couldn't have known." She wound her arms around my shoulders, and her legs around my waist, holding me. I held back a snort. I should be the one comforting her now.

I buried my face in her hair, inhaling deeply, savoring that she was safe and with me. Fuck, I would never let her out of my sight again.

"He threatened me yesterday," I said. "I should have known."

"Rey ..." She pulled back and looked at me. "Don't be so mad about it. If you think about it, Daerman was acting on his feelings. He lost his lover and half of his people because of us. If we were him, we would have done the same." She sighed. "I mean, I wish we were better than this, but in the end we aren't. If something happened to you, I would seek revenge too."

I hugged her tight again. "I can't lose you," I muttered.

She pressed her lips to my temple. "You won't lose me. We'll figure out how to break this curse, we'll fight all of our enemies, we'll set everything right, and the world will be perfect. You'll see."

I smiled. "I love your confidence."

She let out a short chuckle, which sounded almost like a snort. "If only I was confident. I doubt my actions three hundred times a day."

And she was still amazing.

I pulled back and locked my eyes with her. "If you're okay, I should clean the bedroom, then call your mother and tell her what happened."

"Go clean the room," she said. "I'll call my mother."

I nodded. Even this was hard—leaving her to go back to my bedroom. But I forced myself and left her in the kitchen, hopefully only for a short time.

17

ERIN

AFTER A WEEK OF BEDREST, I WAS SICK AND TIRED OF LYING down all the time. With time, I recovered most of my strength, though I couldn't perform magic. Each time I tried, I felt the curse and stopped immediately.

The damn curse prevented me from using my magic, and without my magic, I couldn't perform the Infernal Curse to defeat Brikan.

But just because we couldn't practice magic didn't mean we couldn't practice something. So, I met with my sisters for sword fighting. It was something I really liked, and we didn't need magic for it. Hopefully, we wouldn't need to use swords when the time to fight Brikan came, but if our magic failed, we had a way of defending ourselves.

Jasmin rolled her eyes when she saw me holding my Dawnblade in the center of the combat training room. "Swords, seriously? While you've been in bed, we practiced magic and some fighting skills, but now swords? No, thank you. Call me when you can do magic again."

She stomped out of the room like an angry model on a

runaway, leaving Kristin and me alone. Her sisters had gone to Chasseur Ville to pass the time, and Rey was in the next room, doing some weightlifting.

"What about you? Want to learn sword fighting?" I asked.

"Sure." She shrugged, not sounding too eager.

I sighed. Shit, I was trying. What else was I supposed to do?

Calling my sword, I sat down on the mat and crossed my legs. "Sorry I've been so sick."

She sat down in front of me, mirroring my posture. "It's not your fault."

I knew it wasn't, but I still felt so bad about the problem my condition was causing. My mother had been trying to locate a master curse-breaker since Fiona told her about the curse, but she hadn't found anyone so far.

I rolled my shoulders, trying to let go of those negative thoughts. "You've improved a lot."

She showed me a wide grin. "I've been practicing a lot."

"It shows," I said.

My phone dinged and I frowned. "Sorry, it's my mother asking how I'm feeling."

"You can answer her," Kristin said. "It's nice that you have her and she checks on you all the time."

I tilted my head. "I bet you miss your mother a lot, hm?"

She nodded. "She sacrificed herself for me."

"What do you mean?"

"Honestly, I don't know much, because I was asleep for most of it, but Karen told me that Brikan send a higher demon to our house to kill me, because of the mark. She rushed us out of the house. Karen practically carried me out. And my mother stayed and faced him." She swallowed hard. "She faced him to give me time to escape."

I reached over and held her hand. "I'm so sorry."

"Me too." She inhaled deeply. "Especially because I didn't escape. I got away from Karen and ran back. Karen and Katrina came with me. But we were too late. My mother was already dead."

"And the three of you killed the demon," I said, remembering she had mentioned something about that when we first met.

"Yeah," Kristin muttered. "But we'll make it work, right? I mean, we'll break this curse that is hurting you, and we'll kick Brikan's ass, and I'll have the life my mother wanted for me."

"We will," I told her, trying to believe my own words. "We have to." I tugged her hand and pulled her up with me. "You know, the cafeteria has an ice cream machine. What do you think about sneaking in there and making some ice cream?"

She beamed at me. "I'm in."

I texted Rey, letting him know where we were going—and knowing he would shadow us—entwined my fingers with Kristin's, and together we walked to the cafeteria.

After spending some time with Kristin and bonding a little, something tugged in my chest. I felt the need to check in with my mother.

Rey insisted on walking with me to the Aster building. He halted outside my mother's office, his brows knitted together.

"What's wrong?" I asked.

"Just wondering what you have to discuss with your mother."

"That's the thing," I said. "I don't have anything to discuss with her right now. I just ... thought it would be nice to check on her, you know, like a normal daughter." A little embarrassment heated my cheeks. This was so unlike me, but after hearing Kristin's story about her mother, I realized how lucky I was to have mine right beside me.

His forehead smoothed a little. "That makes sense." He leaned into me and pressed his lips on mine. "Text me when you're done. I'll come get you."

I rolled my eyes, though I did like his overprotectiveness. Most of the time.

Once Rey walked away, I knocked on the door.

"Come in," my mother's voice came from inside. I opened the door and stepped inside. She dropped the papers on her hands and stared at me, a worried knot on her forehead. "Erin? What is it?"

I closed the door and stood there, feeling a little pathetic. "Hm, nothing, to be honest. I just wanted to see if you're okay."

My mother stood up, clearly concerned. "Why? What happened?"

"Nothing happened," I said, approaching her desk. "It's ..." I let out a long sigh. "I just thought we could spend some time together. Not as headmaster and student, or Demon Kissed Queen, but as mother and daughter."

Her gaze softened as she regarded me. "Well, that's surprising, but I'm guessing these papers can wait until tomorrow." She cleared her throat. "How about if we go to my townhouse, and I can cook us dinner while we talk?"

I smiled. "I would love that."

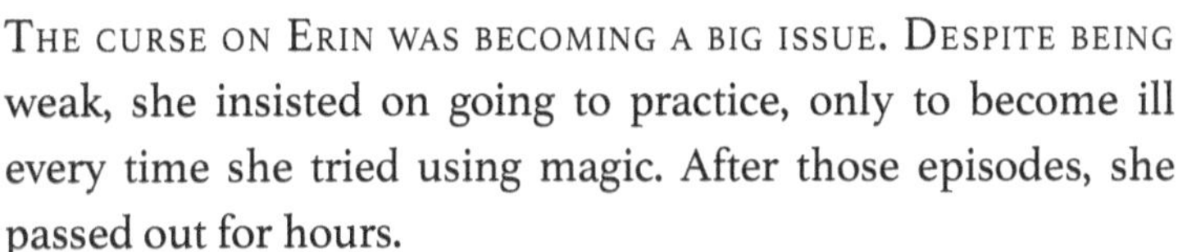

18

THE CURSE ON ERIN WAS BECOMING A BIG ISSUE. DESPITE BEING weak, she insisted on going to practice, only to become ill every time she tried using magic. After those episodes, she passed out for hours.

How the fuck would we defeat the Supreme Demon like that?

Martha continued trying to find a master curse-breaker, and I did too. I reached out to all the demon hunters I knew, and to some demons I knew wouldn't try to bargain with me and send me back to Brikan. But none of them knew any master curse-breaker who was still alive.

Other than that, Claire, Harper, Ava, Harvey, Tanner, and I spent most of our spare time searching the books in the academy—the ones in the library, the ones in the classrooms, in the professor's office, and their townhouses.

One afternoon, we camped at Crimson's house, searching through his hidden collection, except for Ava, who was keeping Erin company—after Daerman's attack, I didn't trust leaving her alone for one second, not when she was too weak to defend herself.

Before, Claire had "borrowed" many from her father, all in time of need—when we needed tracking spells and other things.

"He kept his journals here," Claire said, taking off a big painting from the wall in his office, and revealing a small wooden door with a lock. With the keys in hand, Claire unlocked the door and opened the hidden compartment. The space was full of notebooks. "As I thought. He left in such a hurry, he didn't take any of these." She picked up one journal and skimmed through it.

I picked up another. "What are you looking for in these?"

"Any mention of a master curse-breaker," she said, her eyes on the pages. "I'm sure he must have known one. He always knew everything."

I nodded. Crimson had freaked me out before for knowing things he shouldn't have. "I'll help you."

It didn't take long though. Not five minutes later, Claire let out a huge gasp. Everyone stopped searching through the books and gathered around her.

"What is it?" Tanner asked, looming over her shoulder.

She squirmed, clearly still affected by him. "Hm, from what I understand ... my father is a master curse-breaker."

"What?" I got the book from her and read the page.

In it, Crimson related when a demon hunter was afflicted by a curse, not long ago. The hunter was dying, and no one knew what to do. At first, Crimson didn't do anything, waiting for the others to find a way of breaking the curse, since he didn't want to reveal his knowledge to anyone. But when the demon hunter was drawing his last breaths, Crimson sneaked into his room and performed a complicated ritual, breaking the curse. No one knew how the demon hunter had recovered and the curse had been lifted.

"Wow," Harvey whispered from my side. He was reading the journal with me. "So ... all we have to do is find Crimson."

"Professor, I mean, Headmaster Martha said she tried contacting him after he fled," Harper said. "But she can't find him."

Claire pursed her lips before speaking. "I might know where he is."

Again, everyone stared at Claire, speechless. "We have a beach house in California we usually go to on vacation." She sighed. "He always said he would move there when he got old and needed to retire. I can't be sure, but if I had to bet, I would bet he's hiding there."

I closed the journal. "Then we need to go there."

***

IT TOOK A LOT OF CONVINCING, BUT FINALLY, AFTER PROMISING to be extra careful, Martha allowed us to take one of the school vans and travel to California.

I took the wheel of the van, with Erin seating in the passenger seat by my side. Claire, Harper, and Jasmin took the three seats in the middle, Harvey and Tanner sat in the third row, and Karen, Katrina, and Kristin sat in the last row.

When we started the trip, the air inside the van was tense. Everyone was eager to get this done, but since it was a four-teen-hour drive to California, we needed to be patient.

The drive was normal. There were moments when everyone was quiet, and there were moments when the girls were singing to the songs playing through the speakers, and the guys were teasing them.

Erin joined the singing a couple of times, but even that seemed to make her tired, so she watched with a small smile. My heart tugged every time I sneaked a glance at her. If we were frustrated because of her condition, I couldn't fathom how she felt about it. Actually, we had talked about it many times since it started, but she always shrugged it off, saying that yes, she was upset, but she was sure we would find a solution soon.

We had to.

We really had to.

After seven hours on the road, the sun finally set and the night sky greeted us. I stopped by a roadside inn. "So, who's going to get the rooms, and who's going to get us some pizza?"

Harvey raised his hand and shouted, "I'm going to get the booze!"

19

I waited in the van while Rey went into the inn and rented us a few rooms. One for him and me, one for Claire, Harper, and Ava, one for Harvey and Tanner, and one for Karen, Katrina, and Kristin.

Meanwhile, Claire and Harper went out for pizzas at the shopping mall across the road, and Harvey and Tanner went out for booze.

Thirty minutes later, we all met in Harvey and Tanner's bedroom with the pizza and drinks.

We sat all over the place—the two queen beds, the armchair, and the chair in front of the desk. Kristin even sat on the floor between the beds. The pizza went around, as did the plastic cups with soda, beer, and wine.

We were all eating, mostly quietly, when Ava groaned. "Ugh, it looks like we're heading to a funeral." She grabbed an empty beer bottle. "Here, let's do something fun." She sat down on the floor at the foot of the beds, where the floor-space was wider. "Come on. Everyone on the floor, in a circle."

"I don't want to play," Claire complained, but she sat down between Harper and me.

Though nobody seemed too keen on playing, we all took our places on the floor as Ava wanted, except for Jasmin, who had her feet in the circle, but still sat on the edge of the bed.

"All right, everyone knows how this works, right?" Ava didn't wait for an answer and spun the bottle. The end of the bottle pointed to Katrina, and the mouth pointed at Harper. "There. Katrina, go!"

"Harper, truth or dare?" Katrina asked.

"Truth," Harper said without hesitation.

"Do you like someone?"

Harper nodded. "I do."

Ava whistled. "Who is it?"

Harper took the bottle. "Sorry, one question only." She spun the bottle. It landed on Claire and Jasmin.

"I'm not playing," Jasmin said, getting up and going to the head of the bed. She grabbed a new bottle of beer and sipped from it, looking out the window.

"She's like oil," Harper muttered as she reached for the bottle. She spun again. Once more, it landed on Claire, but this time it pointed at Karen. "Karen, truth or dare."

Karen straightened her back. "Truth."

Claire narrowed her eyes at her. "Why do you hate Erin so much?"

That question shocked me, though I confess, I was curious about it too.

Karen's eyes shifted to me. "I don't hate Erin. I hate the situation, and unfortunately, Erin is involved. I would rather I was the marked one, so I could deal with this myself. I would rather put my life at risk and save them both."

I nodded, my heartstrings pulling hard. "I know what you mean."

"I'm fine," Kristin said. "I want to help any way I can."

"I know, and that's what scares me the most," Karen said.

Silence filled the room.

"All right!" Ava clapped her hands, startling us. "Let's keep moving. Karen, spin the bottle."

She did and it landed on Tanner and Ava.

"Truth or dare?" Tanner asked.

"Truth," Ava replied.

Tanner stared at her, as if he was going to ask her for her soul. "What's the worst thing you've done?"

Ava tsked. "To act like a completely idiot to gain a guy's attention." Her eyes landed on Harvey, who was watching her. The tension in the room went up in flames. With a sigh, Ava spun the bottle. It pointed at her and Harvey. "Truth or dare?" she asked him.

"Dare," he said right away.

Everyone said, "Oooooh!" as it was the first dare of the evening.

"Kiss me," Ava said.

Harvey didn't think. He crossed the space between them on his knees and smacked his mouth on hers. He knelt in front of her, holding on to her as the kiss deepened. We cheered and clapped, except for Karen, who was covering Kristin's eyes.

I thought he would kiss her, and we would go on with the game, but Harvey leaned over Ava even more, and soon the two were sprawled on the floor, kissing nonstop. We all stepped away from them and turned to the rest of the pizza and the drinks.

Karen grabbed Kristin's hand. "It's time for us to go to our room." She gestured to Katrina, who nodded in agreement.

I wanted to tell them to stay, but I knew Kristin was still too young, and with us drinking, and a couple practically going at it in the middle of the room, they should go.

I waved them goodbye, then noticed someone else was missing from the room.

Jasmin.

I took a sip of my wine and handed the plastic cup to Rey. "I'll be right back."

He watched me like a hawk as I left the room and glanced around, looking for Jasmin. I found her at the corner of the inn, her arms crossed over the railing, a beer bottle in hand, looking up the night sky.

"There you are," I said, approaching her.

"If you're here to convince me to go back to that room, don't bother."

"I just want to know if everything is okay."

Jasmin shrugged. "Why do you care?"

I frowned. "Because I'm your sister. Because I'm your friend."

Jasmin snorted. "Friends. I've never had friends."

I leaned on the rail beside her. "Never?"

Jasmin shook her head. "People use me because of my powers, even when they didn't know about them. They knew there was something *wrong* with me. It's always been like that. Until I decided to actually be a succubus and use them instead."

I frowned. "My friends are good people. They would never use you."

"Like you said. *Your* friends."

"They can be yours too, you know," I told her. "All you have to do is let down your walls a little."

Jasmin snorted again. "Right, because it's that simple."

"Then do it with me." I offered her a confident smile. "I'll be your first friend. I'll always have your back, no matter what."

Jasmin squinted at me, as if trying to see past a lie. "Why?"

"Because that's how friendship works. You trust and you're trusted." I bumped my elbow on her arm. "Just give a try."

She rolled her eyes. "Only if you stop bothering me."

I hooked my arm through hers. "That's the thing about friends. They are always bothering you, but in a good way."

I tugged her to come with me. She resisted for half a second, but let me guide her back to the room. To my surprise, Ava and Harvey had disappeared, which only left Rey, Claire, Harper, and Tanner.

I handed Jasmin another pizza slice, and she seemed to relax a little.

We talked, we laughed, we even danced.

It was almost midnight when Rey leaned into me and whispered in my ear, "If you're feeling well, how about we go to our room now?"

I bit on my lip. "I would love too."

He slipped his hand in mine, and without saying good night to anyone, he took me to our bedroom, where, after what seemed like an eternity, we enjoyed ourselves.

20

THE VAN WAS SILENT THE NEXT MORNING, AS IF I WAS ALONE. But that was because everyone was either hungover, or too anxious about seeing Crimson and having this fucking cursed finally lifted.

The weather improved as we drove through California, sending the chills from Colorado away.

Following the GPS's instructions, we arrived at the beach house—a two-story, white contemporary house with many windows. A wide yard stretched in the front, in desperate need of a trim, sliced in half by a long stone driveaway. The beach gleamed in the background, like a teasing bitch. We hadn't come here for that.

I parked the car at the end of the driveaway, and hesitant, we all hopped out of the van. Claire fished the keys from her pocket and unlocked the door.

"What the fuck!" someone shouted from the inside.

We all halted a step inside the house. The place was trashed—pizza boxes, milk cartons, napkins, empty beer bottles littered the living room, hiding from view what looked like sleek furniture. And behind it all, wearing a thin dark blue bathrobe and holding a coffee mug, stood Crimson. His hair was a mess, his beard had grown a few inches, and his eyes were bloodshot.

"Father," Claire said, taking a step closer.

Crimson matched her stride, retreating from us. "Whatever you want, I don't care. Just leave." He pointed to the door behind us.

"Erin was cursed," Claire continued, her voice louder. "We know you are a master curse-breaker. We need you to break her curse. Please."

Groaning, Crimson threw the mug at Claire. The coffee spilled on the floor and couch, and the mug landed right at Claire's feet—it would have hit her legs if she hadn't moved to the side.

"You ... stupid girl!" he shouted. "Why the hell are you here? I left you behind when I ran, didn't I?" He bared his teeth. "You and your shitty friends."

"Father," Claire started.

But Crimson wasn't done. "You disappointed me, did you know that? I never wanted you. Even before you were born, I wished you didn't exist."

Claire went completely still.

A second later, a sob escaped her throat. She ran out, toward the beach. Harper glared at Crimson, then followed her friend.

Erin marched up to Crimson. "I've always wanted to do this." She punched him square in the chin. Crimson's head snapped to the side. "You're a scumbag, the worst of them all."

Crimson turned his evil eyes at Erin, but she didn't give him time to act. She sidestepped him and went after Claire and Harper. I followed her, trusting the others would keep an eye on Crimson.

We followed a wooden path down to the beach, but when we got closer, I held Erin's wrist. "Wait," I told her.

A few yards from us, Claire sat on the sand and Harper sat beside her.

"I'm weak," Claire said, her voice breaking. "I'm useless. I knew he never liked me, but it's one thing to suspect it and another to hear it, to have it thrown in your face." She let out a sigh. "No one wants me."

"That's not true," Harper said. "You're a brilliant demon hunter. You're smart and beautiful ... and I've had a crush on you forever." Claire's eyebrows jumped to her forehead. "I ... I wish you would be my girlfriend."

"Harper," Claire started, swallowing hard. "I never knew you felt that way." She exhaled. "To be honest, I have feelings for you too. I just didn't say anything because I was so hurt after Tanner, I didn't want to get hurt again."

"You like me too?" Harper asked in disbelief.

Claire nodded.

With a smile, Harper leaned over Claire and kissed her.

Erin and I turned, giving them some privacy.

"Yes!" Erin muttered. "Finally!"

I chuckled. "At least one good thing came from this trip."

A moment later, Claire walked by us, stomping her feet on the path toward the house, Harper hot on her heels. We followed them both.

Claire only stopped when she was face to face with Crimson, who still stood in the same spot from before. "You know what? I don't care about what you think. I always knew you didn't like me; I don't even know why I tried. You can go to hell, because I don't need you to feel like I belong. I've found my place."

Crimson stared at Claire, his eyes wide, his jaw slack. I bet Claire had never spoken to him like that before, and that stunned him to silence.

Taking advantage of that, I walked closer. "Here's the deal," I started, drawing his attention to me. "You can help us willingly, or we'll force you to help us. Either way, we aren't leaving this house until you get off your ass and lend us a hand."

Crimson groaned, clearly annoyed. He scanned the room, taking in that we were eleven against one. He would never win against us.

"Fine," he said with a sigh. "I'll do it, just so you all go away."

21

ERIN

CRIMSON DIDN'T WANT OUR HELP SETTING UP FOR THE CURSE-breaking ritual. We watched as he moved the furniture to the side of the living room, making space for a summoning circle.

When I asked him why we didn't do it outside, he said, "I don't want to risk the neighbors seeing anything."

I hadn't paid much attention to the neighbors, but from the little I had seen, they were too close to the house, and there were tall fences separating the lots. Whatever. As long as we got this done, I didn't care where it went down.

After he drew a crude circle on the wood floor with chalk, Crimson told me to step inside.

"I'll need your blood," he said. A moment later, his Dawn-blade appeared in his hand.

Rey stepped forward, but I shook my head at him. I wasn't afraid of Crimson hurting me. He wouldn't, not with so many of my friends around him, ready to exact revenge.

I offered my hand to Crimson. He brought his sword to my open palm, its metal cold on my skin. He pressed the blade down and moved it an inch to the side. I hissed as a tingling pain spread through my hand.

Warm blood pooled at my hand. "What now?" I asked.

"Let it drip down." He stepped outside the circle. "I'll do the rest."

I frowned. "What are we summoning?"

"You'll see," was his answer.

Great. We could be summoning a prince of the underworld for all I knew. Though he was helping, Crimson wasn't being communicative. He offered us the information in parts, as he went with it. Well, if he would do it, the steps didn't matter. Unless it involved my death. Then, we had to rethink the whole thing.

With a sigh, I opened my hand and let the blood drip down to the hard floor. A few steps to the side, Crimson closed his eyes and his lips moved fast as he chanted a spell in a low tone.

Smoke rose from below, as if my blood was acid, eating away the wood. The air around me shimmered.

The lights above head flickered, then went out.

My friends and I tensed, watching and expecting a demon to jump out at any moment.

But no demon came.

White translucent figures descended from the ceiling, floating slowing toward the floor. I gawked at them—six ghosts of both women and men, their hair moving behind them as if they were underwater, their arms open to the sides as if they were flying.

They hovered a foot above the circle.

Crimson's voice became a whisper and I heard a string of words I didn't understand.

I gulped, my eyes on the ghosts—and their eyes on me. "Hm, Crimson. What do I do now?"

"Nothing," he snapped amid his chant. He went on and on, his voice growing louder.

The ghosts held each other's hands, closing the circle. Their translucent figures shimmered and their eyes rolled back.

I felt it then. A jolt of energy pulsated through the floor and came for me. I braced myself, but when it reached me, I didn't feel pain, just a tingle go up my legs to my chest. The tingle spread over me ... then it exploded.

Gasping for air, I fell on my knees.

"Erin!"

"She's fine," Crimson uttered, before continuing the chant.

A moment later, the ghosts were gone, the lights came back on, and Crimson stopped reciting the spell.

"Is it done?" Rey asked.

Crimson nodded. "It should be." He stepped into the circle and watched over me. "So? Is the curse gone?"

With weak legs, I stood. Rey rushed to my side, his hands out in case I fell. Even though I felt a little dizzy, I stood my ground. The curse-breaking ritual had worked, it had to work. And if it worked, I wouldn't feel dizzy anymore, right? This was nothing.

Ignoring the weakness falling over my muscles and my blurred vision, I channeled my magic. The pain started deep in my stomach, but when I cast a darkfire in my hands, it assaulted me, squeezing every inch of me with brutal force.

I gasped and fell.

Rey caught me. He turned deadly eyes to Crimson. "What the fuck did you do?"

"It didn't work?" Crimson asked, his expression bewildered. "It should have. I've used this ritual countless times on me and others."

Rey helped me to the couch, which had been pushed to a wall. I sat down, disappointed. "It didn't work."

"I don't understand," Crimson whispered.

Claire walked up to him and pointed a finger at him. "This isn't over. This might not have worked, but we have to figure out what will, and you'll help."

Crimson glared at her, but didn't argue.

"What's the plan?" Harper asked, her voice soft.

"Let's go to the library," Claire said. "I bet there are plenty of books we can research there."

Ava frowned. "The library? Books about curses in the library?"

Claire rolled her eyes. "The library here." She gestured to an archway that opened up in a long hallway. "Let's go."

My friends trudged behind Claire, all of them on a mission. Crimson groaned, but followed them.

And Rey sat down beside me. "How are you feeling? What can I do for you?"

I offered him a small smile. "Can you break a curse? Otherwise, just stay with me."

"Always." Rey wrapped his arm around my shoulders and kissed the top of my head.

In silence, I held his hand in mine, and through the pain, I stood and tugged him to come with me. We walked down to the beach, and sat down on the sand, watching the waves breaking a few feet from us.

I rested my head on Rey's shoulder. "We have to consider the possibility that this curse will never go away. We need a plan B."

"And what would that be?"

I shrugged, my shoulder pushing on his upper arm. "The only thing I can think of is to make place for a new Demon Kissed Queen."

Rey turned to me, watching me under veiled eyes as if I had sprouted a second head. "What the fuck do you mean?"

"When Cindy and Brianne died, didn't Jasmin and Kristin receive the mark? I don't really know how that worked. Maybe Fiona knows if they got the mark before or after ... Regardless, there were two other girls with the same mark." I looked down at the mark on my wrist. "Maybe if I die, you guys will find a new one."

It was the most logical thing I could think of. Of course, I didn't want to die, but I couldn't fight Brikan this way. If I couldn't fight Brikan, he would kill Jasmin and Kristin, and all of our chances of defeating would be gone. Brikan would be free to imprison the demon hunters and use them to hunt humans instead, just as he always planned.

His nostril flaring with an exasperated exhale, Rey grabbed my shoulders. "Erin, don't you dare think about dying. It's not a noble cause. It's cowardice. We will beat this damn curse one way or another, and you will be the one to kill Brikan once and for all." His gray eyes softened. "And please, never say something like that again. You're my soulmate, Erin, my other half. If you die, I die." He pulled me to him. I sat on his laps, winding my legs around his waist and my arms around his shoulders.

"I love you," I whispered in his ear.

He held me tight against him. "I love you more."

22

EXHAUSTED FROM THE FAILED RITUAL AND TRYING TO USE HER powers again, Erin fell asleep on the beach. I took her inside and set her down at one of the many guest bedrooms.

Then, I joined the others at the library.

Like the rest of the house, the library was a contemporary room with windows from floor to ceiling, but with thick curtains so the sun wouldn't damage the books, sleek glass tables, and many white shelves.

Everyone was seated around the tables, skimming through books, trying to find something about the fucking curse.

"Anything?" I asked as I took a place between Kristin and Claire. I knew the answer, but I had to ask anyway.

Claire lowered the book she had been reading and shook her hair. "Nope."

I let out a sigh and picked up the top book from the pile in front of me. "Then we research some more."

Ava put down her book and narrowed her eyes at me.

"Did you realize that the curse only started after you came back from the underworld?"

I had, but it hadn't been exactly like that. "Actually, it started two weeks after."

Claire tapped her chin. "Tell us about your time with Brikan, if you can, of course. Was there anything odd happening?"

I lowered my gaze, thinking. "There was the ritual ... Brikan promised to bring my mother and sister back from the dead." I wasn't sure if they had been able to see all that after the Shadow Trials with Brikan's barrier up around the arena. "So he started working on a ritual for that."

"And what did the ritual entail?" Harper asked.

I explained to them about the ingredients I retrieve, the pool with the bones, and ... "I drank a potion, and Brikan dropped the rest on the pool."

Crimson's eyes widened. "What were the ingredients in the potion?"

I frowned, trying to remember. There had been so many —some of them went to the potion, and some of them went directly into the pool water. Baby dragon scale, wing of a living bat, mugwort, yarrow ..." I went on, listing all the ingredients.

Crimson pointed a long finger at me. "I know this potion!"

"You do?" Claire asked, in disbelief.

"It's not a potion to raise the dead," Crimson continued. "Brikan could certainly raise the dead without any potions, I'm sure. Those particular ingredients are used for a demonic potion that destroys magic, which can only be created by the most powerful demons."

I frowned. "But ..." I raised my hand to my side and conjured a ball of darkfire. "My magic is fine."

"But Erin's isn't," Tanner said with a gasp.

"Exactly," Crimson said, sounding excited about the discovery. "You weren't the target of the curse, Rey. Brikan used you as a carrier." Crimson's gaze fell to my chest. "Brikan knows you and Erin share a Soul Bond. He must be poisoning her through the bond."

The blood drained from my face, from my entire body. Brikan could have brought my mother and my sister back without any ritual and potions. All along, he was playing me, using me to make the potion that would curse his own daughter, my soulmate. That was why he had let me go in the end. So I would reach Erin and curse her.

My heart sank and I felt sick.

"So ..." Claire jumped up, her chair falling back with a loud thud. "Rey is the one cursed."

Crimson nodded. "And ..."

Claire turned to me, a knowing smile on her lips. "We need to perform the curse-breaking ritual on you."

***

WE LET ERIN SLEEP AS WE SET UP FOR THE RITUAL AGAIN, ONLY this time, I stood in the center of the summoning circle.

Crimson repeated it all—cutting my palm, chanting the spell, summoning the ghosts. An electric jolt traveled through me and I felt it inside my chest—like a cord being stretched, the curse broke and dissolved. Its remains were carried away by the ghosts when they disappeared.

With wide eyes, Crimson approached me. "Did it work?"

"I think so." I looked down at my hands. "I guess we'll only know when Erin wakes up."

"Wake her up now," Jasmin suggested.

It was past midnight. I wouldn't wake her up. In fact, I would join her. I thanked Crimson and everyone for their help, and sneaked into bed with my soulmate.

Erin moved and whimpered as I settled beside her, pulling her to me. Grateful and hopeful, I held on to her as sleep came for me.

THE NEXT MORNING, I WOKE UP BEFORE ERIN BY A FEW minutes. I had just taken a shower and changed into clean clothes when she sat up in bed.

I paused, watching her. "How are you feeling?"

She rolled her shoulders. "Good? I don't know. It's strange. I feel as if the curse is giving me a break."

I nodded. "Erin, please, try to summon your magic."

Her delicate brows curled down. "But you know what happens each time I try."

"I know, but we need to confirm something," I said, my voice careful. Worried.

She looked at me for a moment, considering. She probably noticed I was asking this for a reason, so she inhaled deeply and moved her hand, calling out a bolt of darkfire in her hand.

With huge eyes, Erin stared at the bolt, then at me. "What's going on? Why don't I feel pain?"

I let out a long breath, so relieved. "We found out what happened," I started. I told her about figuring out Brikan had cursed me instead, and performing the curse-breaking ritual on me instead of her. She was as shocked as we had been, but right now, I was just glad it had worked.

Erin jumped on the bed, the bolt of darkfire growing and

becoming a long, dark snake twirling around her. "It's gone! The curse is gone!" She threw herself at me.

With a half-smile, I caught her in my arms. "I'm sorry," I whispered.

Her brow knotted. "Why?"

"Because I was passing the curse to you and I didn't even know it."

"It wasn't your fault, Rey." She placed a kiss on my cheek, then stepped back. "So, now, we get ready to kick Brikan's ass."

She disappeared inside the bathroom for a quick shower. With a satisfied smile, I went around the house, calling everyone.

It was time to go.

23

ERIN

For the next two weeks, my sisters and I trained nonstop. It was clear how much we improved, and we went from killing one lesser demon with our combined powers to killing a handful of neutral demons. We could also deal with two or three higher demons at a time, but anything more than that, and we failed miserably.

Thankfully, Fiona and Rey were always with us, ready to act in case things went awry—and they often did. However, today Rey had a meeting at the Blackthorn Hunters outpost, leaving us alone with Fiona and the demons.

"Remember," Fiona said one day while the girls and I were on a five-minute break. "You need to focus and join your magic if you want to be able to perform the Infernal Curse."

"You keep talking about that curse, but you didn't even tell us what it is exactly," Jasmin snapped.

Fiona pursed her lips. "It's because you're not ready for it yet. You'll only be ready for it when you can join your magic and kill a dozen higher demons without blinking."

Jasmin tsked. "That will never happen."

"If you keep saying that, it won't," Kristin said. It wasn't often that she rebuked Jasmin. It was only when she was really annoyed. As for me, I barked at her all that time, as she annoyed me nonstop. Even after our little bonding time during the trip, Jasmin was still a pain in the ass, but one I forced myself to endure. When she wanted to be, she was pretty cool. The problem was that she never wanted to.

"Enough," Fiona said, her voice rippling with power. "I think the three of you need a longer break." She waved us off. "Come back in an hour."

Jasmin didn't waste time. She practically sprinted out of the training room. Kristin wasn't much different. After a glance at me, she left, probably to go join Karen and Katrina.

I sighed. "Even though we are progressing, we're getting nowhere, aren't we?"

Fiona regarded me with her warm gaze. "I understand your worry, but you need to relax. Your sisters need to relax too. Only then, you'll be able to do what you have to do."

"And what do I have to do?" I asked, knowing she wasn't talking just about combining powers and killing Brikan.

Fiona shook her head. "First, master this." She gestured to the space around us, indicating our training. "Then we'll talk about the rest."

I opened my mouth to complain, but shut it again. Almost every day I asked her to tell me more about the Infernal Curse and the Demon Kissed Queens prophecy, but she never fell for it. I could push all I wanted right now, but I doubted she would tell me.

With a sigh, I whirled on my heels and left the classroom.

Outside, I paused at the stone steps and inhaled the fresh, warm air. It was the first week of April, and finally the weather was losing its chilly touch. The snow around the campus was gone, and I prayed it didn't come back. But who knew? It wasn't unheard of for it to snow in April and even in May in Colorado.

A black raven circled above my head before diving around the side of the Hyacinth building. A moment later, Rey showed up. "Training ended early."

"Fiona was stressed with us and gave us an hour break," I told him.

He stepped to my side and entwined his fingers with mine. "So, what will you do this next hour?"

"Talk to my mother."

As expected, my mother was in her office—the headmaster's office—which once had been Randall's, then Crimson's, and now was hers. It suited her. With her strong personality and perfect posture, it seemed as if she had been born to lead the academy.

Shame the academy was nowhere as glamorous and famed as it once was.

But we would go back to that. Once we defeated Brikan, the academy would be safe again, and there would be more students than ever.

My mother looked at Rey and me. "What is it?"

"A few weeks back, you said we would prepare to go to the underworld," I said, starting the conversation.

My mother frowned. "That was the plan since Rey was there. But Norah got him out, so I don't see why we should go there. That's Brikan's domain. We'll be at a disadvantage."

"When can we go?"

"When you and your sisters are ready to take him down."

I nodded, expecting that exact answer. I cleared my throat, preparing my speech. "I feel like we're running out of time. By now, I'm sure Brikan knows we broke the curse and it isn't affecting me anymore. I'm sure he plans on coming for me, for all of us, soon. But we shouldn't stay here, waiting like sitting ducks. We're putting the students and staff of the academy at risk. He won't expect us to go to them. If we go, we'll catch him unprepared."

"Brikan is never unprepared," my mother said.

"You know what I mean," I said, my voice firmer. "I think we should decide on a date and go."

My mother crossed her arms and leaned back on her chair, her eyes on mine. "Even if I thought that a surprise attack was a good idea, you and your sisters aren't ready. You still can't perform the Infernal Curse."

I threw my hands down. "Because Fiona won't show us how."

"She will show you when you're ready for it."

I gritted my teeth. "What if Brikan comes tomorrow? We still don't know the Infernal Curse." I shake my head. "Knowing the spell isn't the point. When and where we fight is. I want to set a date and go, regardless of everything. Meanwhile, Jasmin, Kristin, and I will work hard on the spell, and we will get it down. But we need to start moving. We don't have an army, we don't have anything right now. If Brikan shows up now, we are all dead."

My mother glanced out the window, thinking.

"Martha, I agree with you that it's imperative Erin and her sisters learn the Infernal Curse, but Erin has a point," Rey said, his voice calm but crisp, like a true professor. "We talked to some demon hunters here and there, but we still don't have enough allies to fight Brikan if he comes. And we all know he won't come alone."

My mother turned her cool gaze to Rey. "What do you suggest, then?"

"We do as Erin says," Rey continued. "We schedule a date, even if in the end we push it back, but it'll give a goal, a reason to push harder. Erin will train more, and the rest of us will put together our own army."

A sigh escaped my mother's lips. She leaned forward on her desk and steepled her fingers. "I'll call a meeting."

***

My conversation with my mother didn't go exactly as I envisioned, but it went well.

An hour later, instead of going back to the training room, Rey and I met my mother, my friends, and Fiona in the largest meeting room in the Aster building. Soon, other people trickled in: professors Genevieve, Astrid, Wesley, Eleanor; and demon hunters Hadrian, Alain, Norah, Doreen, Kaitlin, and Thierry.

When everyone was seated and quiet, my mother started the meeting. "I've called you all here because I've come to a decision," she said, her voice loud and clear. "We'll attack the underworld in ten days." Murmurs spread through the room. "I need to know which of you will go with us."

Everyone raised their hands, except for Alain. My mother didn't call him out on it though.

"Do you think we'll be enough?" Norah asked.

My mother shook her head. "No. We need to call the other hunter outposts and invite them all to come. If you have other allies in the supernatural world, this is the time to ask for their help." She looked at each one of us, a piercing gaze I felt deep in my bones. "This battle won't be easy, and we might fail. But hopefully, we'll rid the world of the biggest evil of all."

The demon hunters clapped and we joined them. We cheered my mother's words, even though deep down worry took root, a worry I had brought on myself.

I only had ten days to master the spells with my sisters, and learn the Infernal Curse.

24

REY

Erin jumped headfirst into her training. Not that she wasn't training before, but now she woke up earlier and stayed at the Hyacinth building until late at night. Thankfully, Jasmin and Kristin understood the urgency of the situation and only complained when they were too tired to stand. Then, the girls took a break, and went right back to it.

One afternoon, I stood at the corner of the room, watching their training, in case the demons went out of control and they needed help. At first, I tried juggling teaching my classes and helping them, but this was more important. Martha assigned my classes to someone else.

Sometimes Tanner joined me, especially when Fiona couldn't come because of previous appointments. She might be a powerful witch, but she was getting old and she had her own life.

One afternoon, the girls were working on adding a fourth higher demon. So far, they had done well with three, but when a fourth was added, they quickly lost control.

On the eighth try, Tanner let out a loud sigh, his eyes on

the girls. "They will kill themselves like this. Not because of the demons, but from exhaustion."

I nodded because that worried me too. But every time I brought it up to Erin, she shut me down. It was one of the few times we ever had a disagreement. So I didn't push it, mostly because I knew I was wasting my time.

"They have to do this," I said, repeating the words Erin had told me so many times these past few days.

"Don't you wonder about the prophecy?" he asked, changing subjects. "There must be a reason why Fiona haven't told us, told *them*, more about it."

I did wonder about that. I wondered about that all the time. "Fiona said she shouldn't tell them more about it, otherwise they would fail."

"See," Tanner said with a bite. "One more reason to be curious, and suspicious, about this entire thing." He frowned. "Isn't Fiona coming back later? We should ask her."

I glanced at the girls—they had subdued two higher demons, but the intense training was taking its toll. They were too tired to be effective. The other two demons advanced on them and they barely had time to react.

Tanner and I stepped forward. I raised a shield of darkfire between the girls and the demons, while Tanner wrapped his magic around the demons. I lowered the shield and helped him, taking the demons by a magical leash to the enchanted and reinforced storage room on the other side of the training room.

The girls sat down on the mat, breathing hard.

My brows curled down. "Why don't you three take a break? Go eat something. Nap, if you need to. Be back here in an hour." I turned to Tanner. "Let's go."

After a glance and a soft smile at Erin, who was lying on

the mat, practically comatose, I walked out of the classroom with Tanner.

"What is it?" he asked as we exited the building.

"Give me a sec," I said, texting Claire. I asked her to stay with the girls while Tanner and I stepped out for a minute. I knew the three of them were powerful, but they were also tired and hot targets at the moment. I knew Claire wouldn't come alone, with at least Harper at her tail, which meant more protection if someone tried to hurt the Demon Kissed Queens.

"What is going on?" Tanner asked, impatient.

I glanced at the time and put my phone away. "Fiona must be arriving any minute now. Let's meet her and talk to her."

Tanner nodded. "I like that plan."

We headed toward the main entrance to the underground garage, where Fiona parked her car every day when she came for training. We climbed down the stairs and scanned the garage. Not ten seconds later, a sedan entered the garage and took one of the visitor spots near the stairs.

Fiona exited the car, a knot in her brow. "What's the matter?"

"Directly to the point," Tanner muttered under his breath.

We waited for her to approach us at the base of the stairs. Then I asked, "Fiona, please, tell us the meaning of the Demon Kissed Queen prophecy."

She shook her head. "I've already told the girls, Rey. I can't tell you."

"That's bullshit!" Tanner snapped.

"Hey." I slapped his chest. "Don't mind him," I said to Fiona. "Why can't you tell us? Because the girls won't continue if you do. That only makes us want to know more."

Fiona let out a long sigh. "Rey, it's not the other girls I'm worried about. It's Erin. She won't want to continue if she knows what the prophecy means."

My heart seized in my chest. "What is that supposed to mean?"

"The three Demon Kissed Queens, daughters of the Supreme Demon, are destined to kill he who shall demand a great sacrifice," she uttered. "That's part of the prophecy's wording."

"So ..." The wheels in my mind spun fast, trying to make sense of what she was saying. "The girls will have to make a great sacrifice." My blood chilled. "Erin will have to make a great sacrifice."

"I've said too much." Fiona shook her head, pressing her lips tight. "But it's true. A great sacrifice, from Erin. If she does not, all will be lost and the supernatural world will be thrown into chaos. King Brikan will rise from the underworld and rule everyone, everything."

I gulped, afraid of my next words. "Erin is going to die, isn't she? That's the sacrifice, right? Her life."

"I can't say more." She started for the stairs, but then stopped at the first step. "It won't be an easy choice, Rey. It'll hurt her, it'll scar her, and that's why she can't know about it now. Just ... stay close to her side and take care of her."

With a last glance full of pity, Fiona turned and went up the stairs.

Once she disappeared on the ground level, Tanner turned to me. "What was that shit about? Erin will die? That's crazy."

It was crazy. It was ... I couldn't think about it. I wouldn't allow Erin to sacrifice her life for us. Because that was what Fiona meant, right? That was why she told me to stay beside

Erin now, because later, Erin would be gone. I understood the concept of sacrificing one life to save thousands, millions even, but I didn't care. I wouldn't let Erin die. I couldn't.

I had to convince Erin to back down from her fight against Brikan.

25

It was the last day before we marched into the underworld, and Jasmin, Kristin, and I still couldn't kill a bunch of higher demons with our combined demons. We had improved, now taking care of five higher demons, with great effort, but it was still not enough.

I had convinced my mother to set a date, she had gotten an army of demon hunters together, and they were all counting on my sisters and me. And yet, despite the countless hours we had trained, we still couldn't do it, and because of that, Fiona hadn't told us how to enact the Infernal Curse.

What bothered me the most was that in the past few days, Jasmin and Kristin had improved so much. Their magic linked as one the moment they started fighting. But mine didn't. It took me a lot of time and effort to join my magic with theirs. I never thought I would be the weak link between the three of us, but here I was, the reason we still didn't know the Infernal Curse. And the thing was, I didn't even know how. After being freed from the curse Brikan had passed on to me through Rey, I had been fine and well, strong even. It should work.

To make things worse, Rey had been acting weird, as if he was hiding something from me. He was still caring and present, always treating me right and being there for me. And at night he cooked for me, and he held me in his bed when I was too sore to do anything more than sleep. But, behind all that, I noticed, in the way sweet way he spoke, in his lingering gaze, in his reverent touches, that he was hiding something. Keeping something from me. I wondered if I should force it out of him, but if he didn't tell me, it was because he wasn't ready yet, or because it wasn't that important. Either way, I knew he would tell me when the time was right, so I waited, pretending I didn't notice anything.

"I'm done," Jasmin said, sitting down on the mat, her breathing fast. "I can't take it anymore."

"Just one more time," I insisted. I glanced at the clock on the wall. It was already seven in the evening. We would be marching into the underworld tomorrow at dawn. I knew we should get a good night sleep, but who was I kidding? I wasn't going to be able to sleep tonight. So it was better if we kept on training. "Please."

Jasmin shook her head, her ponytail swishing side to side. "No way."

"Aren't you two going to Ava's party?" Kristin asked.

I rolled my eyes. Typical of Ava. Early this morning she sent a text to everyone, summoning us for a big party before the final battle. She wanted everyone to relax and have a good time before we all marched to what would probably be our deaths.

Tanner, who had been watching us with Rey at the corner

of the room, approached us with a sly grin. "I'm just waiting for you three to call it quits, then I'm heading there."

"I don't think I'm going," I said, looking at Rey, who made his way to us. "I would rather either train, or sleep."

"You know what?" Jasmin jumped to her feet. "I'm going. This might the last time I drink or dance in my life, so why not?" She shrugged. "I'm out." She sashayed out of the classroom, moving her hips more than necessary, like a top model on the catwalk.

"I think I'm going," Kristin said. "With Karen and Katrina, of course. They wanted to relax a little before ... you know ..." She didn't finish her sentence. We all knew Karen and Katrina were way too worried about her, especially because the two of them weren't trained hunters and wouldn't be going with us.

After a wave of her fingers, Kristin left.

Tanner winked at us. "I'm out to party. See you two later." He also walked out the classroom, leaving Rey and me alone.

Rey reached up and tucked a loose strand of my hair around my ear. "So, you don't want to go to the party?"

I scrunched my nose. "By the time I take a shower, change, apply some makeup, it'll be too late."

Rey slid his hands down my arms and caught my hands in his. "I don't feel like going either, but if you want to, I'll go with you."

I took a step closer to him, even though I knew I was sweaty and stinky. At least he loved me anyway. "I would rather spend this last night with you."

"This last night," Rey whispered, his shoulders dropping. Suddenly, he stiffened, and his gray eyes turned silver with urgency. "Erin, please, I beg you, don't go tomorrow."

I took a step back, making him drop my hands. "What? Where is this coming from?"

"Call off the attack," he continued, a slight tremble in his voice. "Or better yet, let's run. Remember we talked about that before the Shadow Trials. We should do it now. Just pack a few things and go."

I shook my head. "Rey ... what's going on?"

He shut his eyes for a moment and took a deep breath. When he fixed his eyes on mine again, they were full of fear. "Fiona told me you'll have to make a great sacrifice tomorrow. That was what she said she saw in the prophecy, that's what the prophecy means." He erased the distance between us, placing possessive hands on my hips. "Erin, I think it means you'll die. And I won't let you die. I can't ... you can't die."

So that was what he had been hiding from me. He had found out what the prophecy meant, what would come to pass. Even though it wasn't clear, he had assumed I was going to die.

I frowned, not liking this ending. But if it came to that, would I run like a coward and let everyone else face Brikan by themselves? Jasmin and Kristin wouldn't be able to defeat him without me. I couldn't leave everyone—my sisters, my friends, my mothers, the demon hunters—to die in my place.

A lump rose to my throat, but I pushed it down. No, I would stand tall and do what I had to.

If this great sacrifice was my death, then I would deal with it when the time came.

I brought my hand to his face and gently cupped his cheek. "Rey, I want you to forget about the prophecy."

He blinked. "But—"

"At least for tonight, forget about the prophecy. Forget what Fiona told you." I stroked my thumb on his high cheekbone. "I might not want to go to Ava's party, but I would love to party with you. Just me and you."

I slipped my hand from his cheek to his nape and tugged him to me. Rey didn't resist. With a groan, he crashed into me, taking my mouth into his. He wrapped his arms around me and held me against him, as if he could twist us together, a never-breaking single body.

And I hung on to him as he pushed me to the wall and stripped me of my clothes. If this was my last night with him, we had to make it count.

26

REY

ERIN AND I WERE TWO OF THE EARLIEST TO ARRIVE AT THE meeting place—the outside of the cave in the forest behind the academy grounds, where there had been a portal to the academy once upon a time. Erin and I had closed the portal, but Fiona would open it again for us.

Soon, the forest around the cave filled with our friends and fellow soldiers. Martha in full Blackthorn Hunters uniform—sleek, black leather armor with small, green accents. The other hunters—Norah, Andre, Doreen, and Thierry. Ava and Harvey holding hands. Claire and Harper smiling at each other. Tanner rubbing his eyes, looking like he had a bad hangover. Jasmin who, as usual, stared at her nails as if bored. Karen and Katrina, who were escorting Kristin. As far as I knew, they wouldn't cross the portal, but I knew they would stay here with Fiona, waiting and biting their nails.

More and more hunters arrived and joined us.

We might not have the biggest army, but it certainly was fucking strong.

Behind the trees, the sun began to rise.

Martha stopped in front of Erin, Jasmin, and Kristin. "Good luck, girls." She reached for Erin's hand and squeezed tight. "Be careful."

"I will," Erin promised, though her words tugged at my heart. She had tricked me last night. She pushed herself at me, as if I could refuse touching her, making love to her, erasing the troubled thoughts from my mind.

Until this morning, when I woke up and the panic hit me hard, harder than before. I wanted to drop to my knees and fucking beg her to run with me. But I knew better than to ask her that.

Erin would never back down from a fight. And that was one of the many reasons I loved her.

"Everyone ready!" Martha shouted. She glanced at Fiona and gave her a slight dip of her chin.

Fiona raised her hands above her head, calling her magic. She chanted in the witches' language. The cave groaned, as if it was an animal waking up from a long slumber. The ground shook.

Then, orbs of light appeared at the outline of the cave, more and more of them, until they connected, creating a line at the cave's mouth. The light spread, inch by inch, taking over the entire hole.

Fiona gritted her teeth with the amount of power she was juggling with. "It's open. Go!"

Martha took the lead. Erin and I were right behind her.

We marched through the portal, right into the darkness of the underworld. We had come through the portal just outside the archway that bordered Brikan's castle—right where we wanted. I glanced around, but saw nothing more than dark rocks on the ground, the dark mountains in the distance, and the archway to our right.

"This way," I called, as Martha had instructed. Because I had been here, because I had entered his black palace, I would lead us all here.

We entered the archway and followed the long stone path cutting through the red lava lake, the black palace growing bigger and imposing before us.

Although, one thing felt odd—no demons attacked us.

I paused before the black stone steps leading to the castle's main door and closed my fist in the air. Everyone stopped behind me.

"This isn't right," I said in a low voice.

"I know," Erin whispered back. "No one attacked us yet."

"I admit that is odd, but we should celebrate the small things," Martha said. "Let's keep moving."

I glanced at Erin and held her hand in mine for a second.

We went through the door, shoving them open wide, and burst into the castle.

A throng of demons greeted us—muttmaugs, darkelths, and so many others.

"Spread out!" Martha shouted over the clank of metal from the Dawnblades cutting through the demons' flesh, and the grunts and groans coming from our soldiers.

Instantly, Norah went left, and Andre went right, taking most of our army with them. The idea was to clear the palace, while the rest of us went to Brikan's chambers and killed him.

Martha, Tanner, Harvey, Ava, Harper, Claire, Jasmin, Kristin, Erin, and I—we fought our way up the stairs, across the wide corridor, and into Brikan's chambers.

We paused as the doors flew open.

Alone in the center of the first room and in his human

form, Brikan smiled at us. "Well, well, well. I wasn't expecting you so soon." He smoothed the jacket of his suit. "If I knew you were coming, I could have worn something a little more appropriate, don't you think?"

I pointed my Dawnblade at Brikan. "Stop being a motherfucker. Surrender now and we'll kill you mercifully."

Brikan pouted. "Or what?"

Erin and her sisters stepped forward, their heads high. "We'll kill you," Erin said.

Brikan tsked. "Oh, my dear Erin. My offer still stands." He extended his hand toward her. "Join me, and let's take over the world. Together."

Erin rolled her eyes. "Do I really need to answer that?" She called her darkfire. The magic enveloped her hands and her arms like black fire. "Your last chance," she warned.

Brikan's lips stretched in a wide smile. "Do your best."

Erin let out a groan as she threw her hands at Brikan, who didn't move one inch. He stood there as Erin sent several bolts at him.

The bolts zipped past him, through him, and exploded on the wall across the room.

Brikan's body faded away like smoke. His laughter echoed through the room.

"What the hell was that?" Erin asked, her eyes wide.

"An illusion," Martha said, her voice tight.

"You mean ..." My stomach dropped.

"Brikan isn't here," Martha confirmed.

"If he isn't here, then where is he?" Kristin asked, her voice full of determination.

Erin's face paled as realization hit her. "He's at the academy."

27

ERIN

MY HEART BEAT OUT OF MY CHEST AS WE RACED BACK THROUGH the portal, through the forest, and to the academy. Once we crossed the last line of trees and faced the outer northeast wall, we all faltered.

The sun was rising, staining the sky with warm oranges and red—such a perfect view, tainted by one of my worst nightmares.

Demons descended in droves down from the skies, smoke billowed from the buildings, and screams filled the morning air.

"Holy fuck," Rey muttered beside me.

"Let's go!" my mother shouted, raising her Dawnblade above her head.

With renewed purpose, we ran to the academy.

We crossed the gate and joined the fray. With our powers and Dawnblades, we cut through the demons, trying to advance toward the center of the academy.

We found Thierry leading a group of demon hunters at the track behind the Hyacinth building.

"Thank goodness you're here," he panted. His forehead was slick with sweat, and his hands smeared with blood—but not his.

"What happened?" Rey asked, his voice tight.

A muttmaug jumped on Thierry's back, but one of the other demon hunters caught it before the demon caused any damage.

"As soon as you were gone, they just ... appeared," he explained, his eyes round. "They swarmed us and we barely had time to react."

"Where's Brikan?" my mother asked, her face a mask of steel. If she was feeling something with the perspective of finally facing my father, she didn't show it.

"I haven't seen him," Thierry said. "But I heard shouts that he was here. At the Aster building."

My mother looked at me, at Rey, at my friends. "We can't waste any time. We have to cut through these demons. Don't stop for anything, only to take down the demons in our path. Understood?"

Everybody said yes.

"I'll help." Thierry twirled the Dawnblade in his hand. "Guys, clear a path!" he shouted, commanding his group. "To the front of the Hyacinth building! Now!"

The group turned from the track and cut through the demons taking over the path around the Hyacinth building. We followed closely, only attacking when demons came directly toward us.

Once we turned the corner into the Daffodil building, Thierry and his hunters bid us good luck and continued clearing up that side of the academy.

My mother led us through the stone path in between the Daffodil and the Iris buildings. There were few demons here, and a lot of hiding students, surrounded by professors and a few demon hunters.

Karen and Katrina were here with the students, huddling against the stone wall.

Norah was one of them. As we approached her, I saw blood dripping down a nasty cut on her left shoulder.

"How are you holding up?" I asked, tipping my chin toward her wound.

She rolled her shoulders, showing me it didn't hurt too bad. "I'll survive." She let out a long sigh. "Though I can't say the same about the academy."

"Thierry told us Brikan was in the Aster building," my mother said. "Is he still there?"

"Last time I saw him, he was exiting the building," Norah said. "But I don't know where he went after that."

My mother cursed under her breath. "We can't waste time looking for him."

As if answering her, a loud crack split the air, and the ground shook slightly. We glanced around the courtyard.

And there he was.

The Supreme Demon, in his terrible true form, beside the Blackthorn tree.

Fiona and a small group of witches—who the hell were they—stood to the side, throwing their magic at Brikan and the dozens of demons around him, but the king of the underworld easily deflected it all.

My mother glanced at me and my sisters, her eyes hard. "Are you three ready?"

I exchanged a tense look with my sisters. We hadn't mastered the joining of our powers yet, and we didn't know anything about the Infernal Curse. But we would do it. We would find a way. We had to.

I nodded at my mother. "We are."

"I'll help you get there," Norah said.

Professor Genevieve joined our group. "Me too."

"Then, let's go," my mother said, her tone harsh. Ready.

Norah and Professor Genevieve took the lead, opening a path through the demons.

Ava, Harvey, and Tanner darted forward, helping them.

Soon, we reached the edge of the courtyard.

And Brikan saw us.

His lips curled back into a wicked smile, showing off his sharp teeth. "My dear daughters," he said, his voice hoarse, but loud.

In that moment, the battle paused. The demons pulled back, surrounding their king, and the demon hunters spread across the courtyard joined us. They formed a long line beside us, facing Brikan and his demons, their Dawnblades at the ready.

"Call your demons off," I shouted. "Surrender now and die with honor." I didn't even know why I was giving him this option. I knew he would never accept it.

Brikan let out a boisterous laughter. "You really think you can defeat me? That's pathetic. I expected more from you, Erin." He tsked. "If only you had joined me."

"Don't waste your time talking to him," my mother hissed from beside me. "Just attack and be done with it."

Right. Just attack. I inhaled deeply and looked at my sisters. They nodded at me, telling me they were ready.

Without any warning, Jasmin, Kristin, and I raised our arms, calling our magic. We cast a ray of darkfire—a single one—and shot it at Brikan.

He laughed again as shadows bubbled from the ground in

front of him. Four shadows, to be exact, quickly formed into four men.

"The princes," Rey whispered beside me.

The princes united their forearms, closing all access to Brikan. Our darkfire ray hit them and was absorbed, as if we were pouring water on a sponge.

The battle resumed.

My sisters and I kept trying to break through the princes, while Rey, my mother, my friends, and the demon hunters attacked the demons surrounding the king in the courtyard. Though I didn't want to get distracted, it was hard not to keep tabs on Rey, who was advancing toward the princes, closely followed by my mother.

Shit, I knew Rey was a powerful half-demon; after all, he was the son of a prince of the underworld. But damn, going head to head with four princes? He was out of his mind.

"This isn't working!" Jasmin screamed, bringing my mind back to my own mission.

Our power was flying too fast, and we were draining ourselves—of magic and stamina.

"Keep going, girls," Fiona said, coming to stand besides us. "We'll help you." Fiona and her witches joined my sisters and me, using their own magic to weaken the princes.

Two of the princes turned, leaving their formation. No doubt, Rey and my mother had engaged them in a fight. I pressed my eyes shut for a moment and focused.

"It's too hard," Kristin said, through gritted teeth.

"Keep going!" Fiona instructed. "We've almost broken through."

A prince turned away, following Norah's and Genevieve's taunts.

All right. Just one prince. "We can do this!" I shouted, forcing more of my power into the stream of darkfire.

The prince didn't stand there, waiting to be obliterated. With the others gone, he couldn't absorb all of our power.

So he attacked.

He came at us, baring his fangs.

"More!" Fiona screamed.

We sent more power. The ray of darkfire grew thicker, darker. It hit the prince in the chest, delaying his advance. The prince's skin started glowing orange. First his hands, then his neck, and last his face. We held the spell as the prince burned from the inside out. His body trembling, he fell to his knees. His skin charred, and a terrible burnt smell reached my nose. With a last gasp, the prince's body crumbled like ashes.

The spell broke.

The girls and I leaned forward, our hands on our knees, breathing hard.

One down. Three to go.

Thankfully, when I straightened my back and glanced up, I only saw one prince standing. One had been killed by Rey, my mother, Claire, and Harper. Norah, Genevieve, Ava, Harvey, and Tanner had killed the other.

All of us turned to the last one, but before my sisters and I could send our magic to him, the others joined their forces and killed him.

But not before the prince impaled Professor Genevieve with his long claws. My chest tightened in shock and rage, but I didn't have time to mull it over. As if we had choreographed it, Rey, my mother, my friends, and the others formed a corridor between Brikan and us, keeping the rest of the demons away.

My sisters and I faced Brikan.

My stomach sank.

The Supreme Demon looked every bit as demonic and powerful, standing in front of the Blackthorn tree, reaching halfway up its long trunk with his height. The horns curled around his big head, and his eyes shone bright with pure death.

Brikan shook his big head. "I guess playtime is over."

He raised his hands, probably to strike us.

My sisters and I did the same, but before we could join our powers, Fiona pointed at him. "Now!"

The witches bombarded Brikan with their magic, while Fiona stepped closer to me. She closed her hand around my wrist and said, "It's time. You'll perform the Infernal Curse and the Demon Kissed Queens prophecy will come to pass."

My brows knotted. "What do you mean?"

My mother walked to us. "I'm ready."

My frown deepened. "What are you talking about?"

"The Infernal Curse can only be performed after each of you sacrifice something precious to Brikan," my mother said, her voice oddly kind.

"I don't ..." My mind spun. What were they talking about?

"Jasmin and Kristin lost their mothers to Brikan," Fiona said. "They sacrificed themselves to save their daughters."

I looked from Fiona to my mother, the words sinking in.

"No, no, no." I clutched my mother's arm as my chest tightened. "You can't do that. You can't. I can't ..." A sob broke my throat. "I can't lose you."

My mother patted my hand in her arm. "You won't lose me. I'll always be with you."

I shook my head, my vision blurring with tears. "There has to be another way."

"There isn't, Erin," my mother said. She pulled my hand from her arm. With a soft smile, she leaned into me and pressed a kiss on my forehead. "Remember, I'm so proud of you. I love you, Erin."

Then she was gone.

Fiona held on to my hand as my mother turned and rushed Brikan. Knowing exactly what to do, the witches drew their spells back. My mother jumped Brikan and pushed him back, until his back hit the Blackthorn tree.

"Now, this is the Infernal Curse," Fiona said. "Join your powers and send the darkfire at the tree." The girls acted right away, but all I could was stare as my mother struggled with Brikan. He was playing with her, letting her think she was winning. How terrible it must be for her, to be facing him at this moment, after he'd tricked her over twenty years ago. Fiona shook my shoulder. "Erin! Now!"

I snapped out of it.

Not trusting myself, I just acted. I merged my magic with my sisters', and our darkfire infused the tree. A few seconds later, the tree shuddered and its trunk grew. The black trunk of the tree wrapped around Brikan's body, trapping him in the tree.

Caught by surprise, he roared, his power rippling out in a big wave. We ducked, missing its hit by an inch. But others hadn't been fortunate. Several hunters fell down, either passed out or hurting.

And my mother's body fell on the ground at Brikan's feet.

I stopped breathing.

"No, don't close up yet," Fiona said, placing herself in my line of sight. "It's almost done. Focus!" I turned my eyes to hers, though I wasn't seeing much. "Erin, summon your

Dawnblade." I did, the sword appearing in my hand with a single thought. "Girls, here's what you have to do."

I didn't listen. I was too deep in myself, lost to dark thoughts, rage, and grief. I dragged my feet along with Jasmin and Kristin as they advanced toward a jerking, screaming Brikan.

Someone dragged a body to the side as the girls and I took the last few steps, before halting in front of the Supreme Demon.

He spewed some nonsense, but my mind was too addled for me to understand.

Until he said, "Martha deserved it! It was so easy to trick her when she was young. And she seemed to be just as stupid now!"

Oh, that did it.

Suddenly, all of Fiona's words made sense and I snapped out of my trance. I held on to rage as I lifted the Dawnblade. Jasmin and Kristin wrapped their hands around the hilt with mine, and we infused the sword with our darkfire—all of it, all we could.

Then, we plunged it into Brikan's chest.

The magic exploded ... everywhere. In our hands, our arms, into the demon, through the tree, in the air around us. It was so strong, it sent the three of us skidding back a couple of feet.

Then, it all stopped and we watched the Supreme Demon as he gasped, his fang-filled mouth going slack. His eyes rolled back. Next, his body started shimmering, until it too became ashes at the roots of the Blackthorn tree. Still alive with our power, the tree grew a little more, raising one of its thick roots and scooping the ashes into the earth.

King Brikan was dead.

Erin stood in front of the Blackthorn tree, holding her mother's Dawnblade.

The aftermath of the battle against Brikan hadn't been pretty. After Erin and her sisters killed the Supreme Demon and the tree got rid of his remains, the other demons either perished at our hands or fled. Amid the battle, the students were escorted to their dorms and told to stay there for the time being. When the demons were all gone and the campus was deemed safe, most students left, saying they would never return to the academy again.

I couldn't blame them for feeling that way.

Unfortunately, we had lost a few students, professors, and demon hunters during the battle. Of our friends, Harper had injured her arm, Harvey had been stabbed in the stomach, but would be all right, and Norah had wounded her shoulder. Everyone sported bruises and weariness, but we would be all right.

Yesterday, two days after Brikan's death, Erin sat down with Jasmin, Kristin, and Tanner. They officialized their previous deal—Tanner would head to the underworld, accompanied by a great number of demon hunters, in case there were any demons still hanging around, and take over the throne. Jasmin would go with him, and they would establish later what part of the underworld belonged to her. She would be the first princess of the underworld. Erin and Kristin also became princesses of the underworld, with enough power to overthrow Tanner in case the power went to his head, and he became a motherfucker like Brikan. Kristin left with Karen and Katrina, promising to keep in contact.

And I ventured into Brikan's castle when Tanner went down there, and retrieved my mother's and my sister's bones, which now were buried in a small marked grave beside Martha's resting place—under the Blackthorn tree.

Heavy clouds rolled in the skies, darkening the day. Soon, it would start raining.

"Do you want to say something?" I asked Erin, knowing this was her own funeral for her mother.

She shook her head. "I don't know what to say," she whispered.

I hooked my arm around her shoulders and pulled her closer to me. "I'm sure she knows how you feel about her."

Erin's golden eyes filled with tears. "I hope so."

We stayed there, quiet but together, saying our goodbyes to our families. I felt rather relieved that I could now visit my mother's and sister's graves more easily. I had really missed them.

My phone vibrated in my pocket. I fished it out from my pocket and saw the text message.

Harvey: They are arriving. You better come.
Me: omw.

"Erin, we should go," I told her, pocketing my phone again.

"I know," she whispered. She knelt on the marked grave and inserted the Dawnblade in the little fissure on the headstone, which had been left for this purpose. "I'll see you later, Mom."

Erin stood up and faced me. "Let's go."

I entwined her fingers with mine, and together we walked to the Aster building.

ERIN

LONG AGO, I CAME TO REALIZE NOT ALL SUPERNATURALS WERE evil. After so many battles, the other demon hunters were starting to see that. So when I proposed we set up a meeting with some of the leaders of the supernaturals—the ones we knew, at least—to talk about the future of the supernatural community, most Blackthorn Hunters were skeptical, but they agreed to it.

Now, the largest meeting room in the Aster building held the most powerful beings in the world. Thea, the Witch Queen of the Silverblood coven; Drake, the lord of the DuMoir Castle; Luana, the alpha of the Starlight wolf pack; Keeran, the Warlock Lord; their right hands: witch Elisa, vampire Cain, werewolves Romulus and Meira, warlock Aspen; the Witch Queen of the Blackmarsh coven, Queen Sarah; the Witch Queen of the Bluemoon coven, Queen Rosilla; the Witch Queen of the Bonecrown coven, Queen Corvina; the Witch Queen of the Wildthorn coven, Queen Yira; witches Fiona and Acalla, both of whom possessed prophecy powers; Lark, the fae prince living in the human realm, the same one Farrah was running from when I met her; General Auron, Prince Lark's man, who was now glaring daggers at me; the main group of the Blackthorn Hunters: Alain, Hadrian, Norah, Andre, Doreen, Kaitlin, and Thierry; the academy professors: Eleanor, Genevieve, Astrid, Wesley, Vander, Adeline.

Of course, as my personal team, Claire, Harper, Ava, and Harvey—with a thick bandage around his middle —joined us.

For this meeting, even Tanner, the new king of the underworld, and my sisters, Jasmin and Kristin, had come back.

It was intimidating to face all of these powerful supernaturals right now and lead this meeting.

"I called all of you here today because I believe times are changing," I started, as I had practiced with Norah this morning. I had been nervous about this topic, especially with Alain and Hadrian at the meeting, two big-name demon hunters who probably wouldn't like what I had to say. "We know now that not all supernaturals are evil. I know that all of you here aren't evil. Which means the rules of the Blackthorn Hunters need to change."

As I expected, Alain was the first to open his mouth. "Who made you owner of the Blackthorn Hunters?"

"Alain, shut up," Norah snapped. She had been stiff since she first walked into the room, and I noticed her and Cain, the vampire prince from DuMoir Castle, exchanging heated glances. A few months ago, Rey told me that Cain had asked about her when he came with Thea and Drake to retrieve the witches we had saved from Randall. Was there something going on there? "Erin and her sisters just killed Brikan and cleared out the underworld. I say we hear what she has to say." She nodded at me, silently telling me to continue.

I swallowed and went on, "The academy should now train the demon hunters students to not only hunt and kill demons and supernaturals, but first to recognize if they are evil or not. If they aren't, then the demon hunters will leave them alone. If they are ... then, they will be dealt with accordingly."

Murmurs of agreements spread through the room.

"I have a question," Professor Astrid said. "Will we continue to teach both demon hunters and half-demons?"

"Actually," Jasmin started, taking over. "I already talked to Erin and Rey about this and both of them agreed with me. I'll set up an academy for the half-demons in the underworld." She glanced around in a teasing way. "Professor positions are now open."

Some chuckled, some groaned. But at least no one voiced any disagreement.

"I like that," Thea said. "When I met Rey a few months ago, he told me about the academy for demon hunters, and I became intrigued. After researching and preparing, I can now announce that I'm setting up an academy for witches close to the Silverblood Estate."

"That's a great idea," I said, remembering again all those witches we saved from Randall's clutches. Now Thea could not only give them a home, but also teach them proper magic.

"We should discuss setting up an academy for mixed supernaturals," Acalla suggested. "Vampires, werewolves, fae—"

"Leave fae out of this," Prince Lark snapped. He tugged on the dark cloak over his shoulders.

Acalla frowned at him. "Why? We should try to integrate all supernaturals—"

"Fae are almost god-like," Lark said, interrupting the

witch. "Do you think we want to mix up with others?" He glanced around the room, disgust clear in his dark eyes. "You know what? I shouldn't even be here." He gestured for General Auron, and the two of them marched out of the room.

I stared at the door for a second, stunned by his superior attitude. Holy shit, this was the guy that Farrah was promised to marry? I was glad she was on the run from him. Hopefully, he would never find her.

I cleared my throat. "All right, that is that," I said, moving on. "We should talk more about this mixed supernatural school. It's definitely a good idea."

"Speaking of academies, how about we focus on this one for a moment more?" Professor Eleanor said. "Like, we don't have a headmaster anymore. Who will run this academy?"

"Rey!" Norah said, without hesitation.

Beside me, Rey stiffened. "What? No!"

"I second that," Thierry said, surprising me. With our brief past, I thought he kind of hated Rey's guts.

Andre nodded. "Thirded."

The idea spread like wildfire, and soon everyone was agreeing that Rey was the best candidate to take over the mantle of headmaster of the Blackthorn Hunters Academy.

"Just accept it, Rey," Norah insisted. "You are the best person for the job."

I glanced at him. "How do you feel about it?"

He stood taller, like a powerful headmaster. "I'm fucking stunned, but also honored. If you really believe this is the right path—" His eyes scanned the crowd. "—then I accept it."

"Congratulations, Headmaster Rey," I said with a smile.

We talked about a few more details—what to do with the

rest of the semester, about campus security, the new academies, etc.—then we moved on to the dining room, where we could celebrate new beginnings.

As headmaster, Rey sat at the head of the table, and I sat to his right. The food was served, the drinks were passed around, chatter spread, laughter echoed.

I glanced at everyone at the table—demon hunters, half-demons, witches, vampires, werewolves ... everyone fraternizing as friends. This was the world we needed right now.

Across the table, Rey took my hand in his, entwining our fingers. "Is this what you imagined?"

I smiled at him. "It's even better."

And with him by my side, I was sure everything would be even better from now on.

ONE YEAR LATER

REY

"ERIN BELMONT," I CALLED FROM UP THE LITTLE STAGE SET UP at the base of the Blackthorn Tree.

Erin, who had changed her fake last name to her mother's one, stood from her seat and walked to the stage. Amid the applause of the other students, professors, and family members, she stepped onto the stage and halted in front of me.

With a smile, I handed her the diploma. "Congratulations, demon hunter Erin."

I extended my hand to greet her. Erin rolled her eyes as she slipped her hand in mine, but to my surprise, she stepped into me and pressed her lips to mine. I chuckled, because we had talked about this. I was the fucking headmaster now, and she was a student. Though everyone knew we were together, we had tried to keep the PDA to a minimum in the past year —a very hard task.

"What?" She shrugged. "I'm not a student anymore."

She hopped off the stage and high-fived Ava on her way back to her seat.

Feeling lighter and happier than ever before, I continued with the graduation ceremony, calling the students, including Claire, Harper, Ava, and Harvey, and handed them all their diplomas.

Once the official ceremony was done, the chairs were pulled aside and a big party started. Loud music filtered from the speakers spread around the courtyard. Food and drinks had been brought out from the cafeteria. Friends and family danced and talked and laughed.

And I took my beautiful soulmate to the improvised dance floor. I held her against me, loving how her body easily molded around mine. It was like she had been made for me.

"I'm proud of you," I whispered in her ear.

Erin pulled back and glanced at me with her bright golden eyes. "What's that for?"

I lifted my shoulder. "Everything. Many obstacles were thrown in your way, but you never steered off the right path. You stayed strong, beat up the biggest evil of all time, and now you are a true demon hunter."

Although Brikan was gone, and Tanner was leading the underworld with firm hands, on the right path, there were still demons in the world. And now that they couldn't hide in the underworld, the attacks on humans had been more frequent, more chaotic. Demon hunters were needed now more than ever.

"Well, I'm proud of you too," she said. "I know it's been only a year, but so far, you've been a great headmaster."

I smiled at her, glad she wasn't mad at me for the hours I had to work this past year to make the academy more secure, to hire more professors, and to bring back the students who had fled when things started going array. Thankfully, enrollment was rising, and everyone seemed excited to be here.

I caught Erin glancing around, her gaze pausing at specific people. Tanner and Jasmin were seated at the edge of the courtyard, with glasses of champagne, talking business as usual. Karen and Katrina had brought Kristin since she had begged to come for Erin's graduation. The three of them were dancing with Claire and Harper, who held hands, showing off their love for everyone, and Ava and Harvey. Ava moved her left hand more than necessary, just to show off the big ass diamond shining on her finger—Harvey had proposed last night.

Although this was the end of an important phase in their lives, it wasn't over. Erin, Ava, and Harvey were joining the nearest Blackthorn Hunters outpost, a few miles from the academy. Claire was going to assume the mantle of Demon History professor, and Harper, who was studying magic more and more, would open a magical trinkets shop in Chasseur Ville.

Life might change for all of us, but I was sure we would stay connected. Erin would make sure of it.

We danced with our bodies pressed together, laughed with our friends, drank a little, until the party wound down.

I slipped my hand into Erin's. "Come with me," I told her.

I brought her to the underground garage.

She raised her eyebrows. "Where are we going?"

"You'll see," I said, opening the door of my car to her. Wary, she climbed in.

And I walked around my car and took my seat behind the wheel.

I exited the academy and turned down a small dirt road a mile out. I followed the road as it cut through the forest, until it opened up to a small, contemporary-style chalet at a lake's bank.

As soon as I stopped the car, I hopped out. Erin slowly got out, her eyes wide at the chalet. "What's this?"

"Our house," I said, simply, walking to her.

It took a moment for the words to sink in, then Erin's jaw fell open. "W-what?"

I halted beside her, letting her take it all in. I had found this chalet almost ten months back, and it had taken a few months to restore it and transform it into a more contemporary style. The first floor walls were of thick gray stone, but the top floor was ninety percent glass, with wood frames here and there. A huge back porch opened to the lake with two chaise lounges, where I imagined Erin and me relaxing together with a glass of wine after a long day.

The chalet was halfway from the hunters' outpost and the academy, which meant we both could be here after work hours. And if there was an emergency, we could go back in a few minutes.

It was the perfect place for us.

I inhaled deeply, measuring my next words. I had thought about presenting her a ring along with the chalet, but when Harvey started talking about proposing to Ava right before graduation, I didn't want to seem like a copycat. Besides, Erin was my soulmate. We already had something that showed we belonged to each other—the Soul Bond mark on our chests.

"I bought it for us," I told her. "If you like it, then this is now our home."

She turned her perfect smile at me, her golden eyes brighter than normal with unshed tears. "I like it. I love it." She hooked her arms around my shoulders. "I love you."

I leaned into her and pressed my lips to hers. "I love you more," I said, before taking her mouth and kissing her deeply.

I had lived a long enough life to know that things wouldn't be perfect from here on out, but I also knew that happiness was in the small things. In Erin's smile, in her hand in mine, being by side, talking to her ... Right now, I couldn't imagine being any happier.

And I knew that together we would overcome anything life threw at us.

THANK YOU

Thank you for reading *The Infernal Curse*!

Reviews are very important for authors. If you liked my book, please consider leaving a review on your favorite retailer and/or on goodreads, please!

Did you like this book? You can check out other books of mine. You can find direct links to all of my books on my website!

The Vampire Heir (Rite World 1: Rite of the Vampire): a dark and mysterious paranormal romance about a vampire and a young woman with a secret.

The Warlock Lord (Rite World 4: Rite of the Warlock): a thrilling and kick-ass paranormal romance about a werewolf and warlock.

Heart Seeker (The Fire Heart Chronicles book 1): an urban fantasy series about a young woman who finds herself at the center of a mysterious supernatural world.

Destiny Gift (The Everlast Series book 1): a post-apocalyptic urban fantasy series about a young woman with a special power that can save the world.

Don't forget to sign up for my Newsletter to find out about new releases, cover reveals, giveaways, and more!

If you want to see exclusive teasers, help me decide on covers, read excerpts, talk about books, etc, join my reader group on Facebook: Juliana's Club!

ABOUT THE AUTHOR

While USA Today Bestselling Author Juliana Haygert dreams of being Wonder Woman, Buffy, or a blood elf shadow priest, she settles for the less exciting—but equally gratifying—life as a wife, a mother, and an author. She resides in North Carolina and spends her days writing about kick-ass heroines and the heroes who drive them crazy.

Subscribe to her mailing list to receive emails of announcement, events, and other fun stuff related to her writing and her books: www.bit.ly/JuHNL

For more information:
www.julianahaygert.com

facebook.com/julianahaygert

twitter.com/juliana_haygert

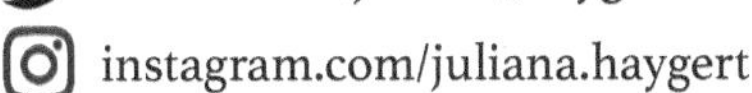

instagram.com/juliana.haygert

ALSO BY JULIANA HAYGERT

To find links and more info, go to:

www.julianahaygert.com/books/

Shorts

Into the Darkest Fire

Tested

Rite World: Blackthorn Hunters Academy

The Demon Kiss (Book 1)

The Hunter Secret (Book 2)

The Soul Bond (Book 3)

The Shadow Trials (Book 4)

The Infernal Curse (Book 5)

Rite World

The Vampire Heir (Book 1)

The Witch Queen (Book 2)

The Immortal Vow (Book 3)

The Warlock Lord (Book 4)

The Wolf Consort (Book 5)

The Crystal Rose (Book 6)

The Wolf Forsaken (Book 7)

The Fae Bound (Book 8)

The Blood Pact (Book 9)

The Wyth Courts

Winter King (Book 1)

Spring Warrior (Book 2)

Summer Prince (Book 3)

The Fire Heart Chronicles

Heart Seeker (Book 1)

Flame Caster (Book 2)

Sorrow Bringer (Book 3)

Earth Shaker (Novella)

Soul Wanderer (Book 4)

Fate Summoner (Book 5)

War Maiden (Book 6)

The Everlast Series

Destiny Gift (Book 1)

Soul Oath (Book 2)

Cup of Life (Book 3)

Everlasting Circle (Book 4)

Willow Harbor Series

Hunter's Revenge (Book 3)

Siren's Song (Book 5)

Breaking Series

Breaking Free (Book 1)

Breaking Away (Book 2)

Breaking Through (Book 3)

Breaking Down (Book 4)

Standalones

Daughter of Darkness